Sarah Greene and the hostages ran for their lives at the cliff's edge as the heat from the volcano steamed up over them. A burst of weapons fire from behind them threw them to the ground. Sarah saw one of the Samurai charging toward them. Dodging bullets, waving a sword, he was coming straight toward the girls. He screamed, "BANZAI!"

Sarah scrambled to her feet and threw herself in front of him. It was like trying to stop a train. He plowed into her and kept on going, driving her backward until she stood, struggling for balance, inches away from a plunge into the molten lava. . . .

Also in the TALON Force Series

THUNDERBOLT
MELTDOWN
SKY FIRE
SECRET WEAPON

TALON FORCE

ZULU PLUS TEN

Cliff Garnett

A SIGNET BOOK

SIGNET
Published by New American Library, a division of
Penguin Putnam Inc., 375 Hudson Street,
New York, New York 10014, U.S.A.
Penguin Books Ltd, 27 Wrights Lane,
London W8 5TZ, England
Penguin Books Australia Ltd, Ringwood,
Victoria, Australia
Penguin Books Canada Ltd, 10 Alcorn Avenue,
Toronto, Ontario, Canada M4V 3B2
Penguin Books (N.Z.) Ltd, 182–190 Wairau Road,
Auckland 10, New Zealand

Penguin Books Ltd, Registered Offices:
Harmondsworth, Middlesex, England

First published by Signet, an imprint of New American Library,
a division of Penguin Putnam Inc.

First Printing, August 2000
10 9 8 7 6 5 4 3 2 1

People sleep peacefully in their beds at night only because rough men stand ready to do violence on their behalf.

—George Orwell

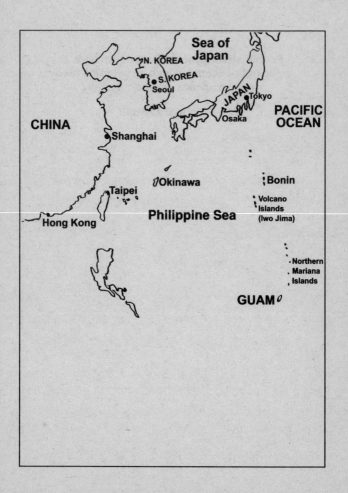

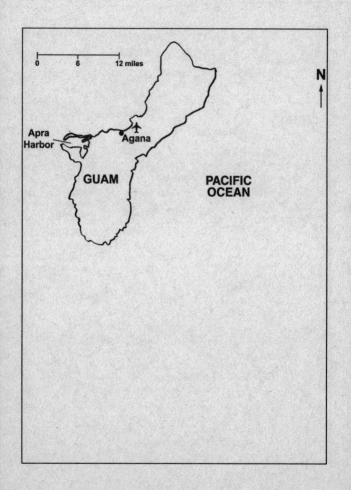

Prologue

August 1, sunrise,
a remote island in the Pacific

At least the girls were drugged. If they hadn't been, he might have tried to save them, the odds be damned. But they were beyond help now; and without his report more of them would surely die. As the ceremony proceeded, he resisted the urge to interfere.

The solitary drum beat a steady cadence as four samurai carried the altar to the volcano's edge, the others bowing as the procession passed. Heat waves rose from the caldera and the sulfur-tinged air shimmered. The sound of the surf pounded in his ears. The sky was reddening in the east. A Shinto priest—a wizened old man, his black hair shot through with gray—stepped forward and unfurled the sacred cloth. With gnarled hands, he smoothed it carefully over the altar's edge.

The shogun stepped forward and the crowd hushed. In his ceremonial headdress, with red robe fluttering in the sea breeze, he seemed larger than life—more god than man. The witness swallowed. If evil walked the earth, he thought, then truly it was here.

The guards stepped forward and pulled the girls to their feet. Even doped, their eyes were wide with fear. One by one the maidens were unbound, stripped naked, and displayed for the men. A collective stir of anticipation went through the crowd.

With a wave of his hand the shogun made his choice. The maiden was placed on the altar. The crowd stilled. In the silence, the molten stomach of Suribachi-yama growled.

The shogun lifted his robes and mounted the girl. Clawing the air, her eyes wild, she struggled as the guards held her fast. The witness closed his eyes. He had not been prepared for this. How old was this child? Thirteen? Fourteen? Undoubtedly a virgin. He thought of his own little girl and his jaw clenched. He wanted to kill the shogun, take him by the throat and squeeze until his windpipe snapped. Instead, the man placed a hand on his chest and felt the hum of the tape recorder, the wires running from it to the mini-camera on his collar. This time, no one would be able to call him a liar. This time, they would have to believe him.

I will put a stop to this.

It was finished. The girl rolled off the table, blood running down between her legs, and scrambled drunkenly to rejoin the others. The shogun adjusted his robes and regained his seat, then nodded toward the first row of men.

The witness had been selected for the first row today—it was an honor—but had cunningly traded places with another. As his camera rolled, the chosen men fell on the girls, raping them repeatedly while they cried out for mercy. In his chair on the sidelines, a look of contentment settled on the shogun's face. Today's sacrifice would buy ten more years of power from the volcano god.

The men's lust had been satisfied, but Suribachi-yama's had not. As the witness watched, the girls were lifted onto the men's shoulders and hurled into the fiery pit, their screams drowned out by the cheer of "*Banzai!* Ten thousand years!"

It was time to leave. Tomorrow, the man would go to the Japanese authorities and they would put the perpetrators in jail for their crimes. But first, he would go home and kiss his wife and his children. And never, ever would he tell them what he had witnessed. Already, the memory of it felt like a stain on his soul.

The altar was dismantled and the samurai fell into formation to begin the long trek back down to the black sand beach. They had to step carefully to avoid the steam vents that pockmarked the island, spewing vapor that smelled like the devil's own breath. By the time the sun was fully up, this place would be as it had been. No evidence of the sacrifice would remain.

A quarter mile away he saw the ship, all but invisible where it was anchored in the tiny bay. The man's mouth felt dry and his fingertips were cold. Why should he be so nervous now, when victory was within his grasp? He must stay calm. Everything was going as planned.

Suddenly, the line stopped. No one said a word as they stood, eyes front, waiting for instructions. The man swallowed. What was holding things up? He shifted subtly and peered down the line of bodies. What was going on?

His heart froze. One by one the men were being frisked, patted down before they boarded the skiff. His mind raced with a thousand questions. What were they searching for? Had someone tipped them off? Had his cover been blown? Or was this just a routine check?

Routine or not, it was a disaster. A thorough pat down would reveal the electronics beneath his tunic as surely as an X ray.

His heart pounded in his ears. There was no way to get onto the ship without being searched and no way to avoid a search without arousing suspicion. He would have to remove the recording devices and leave them behind. He could return for them later. Suribachi-yama would not demand a sacrifice for more than a month; there would be plenty of time to get the evidence.

He knew what he must do.

Leaning forward, the man clutched his belly and moaned. The column moved to the side, but no help was offered as he retched violently and staggered toward an outcropping of yellowish, lichen-covered rock. His plan was simple: get out of sight long enough to remove the incriminating evidence then rejoin the group. Nausea was a convenient excuse and one that no one would question. Even a samurai could have a weak stomach. It was a good plan. And it almost worked.

But as the man lifted his tunic, the old Shinto priest came around the boulder looking for a place to relieve himself. At the sight of the wires and boxes strapped to the traitor's chest, his face turned purple and he began sputtering angrily.

The man dropped the recording devices and sprinted down the hill, lurching clumsily as his sandals slipped on the volcanic rock. He could hear other voices behind him. Angry voices. As he scrambled down the leeward side of the island, a hundred footsteps followed.

What now? Even if he made it to the water, how would he get away? There were no other ships here, no people who could help. The grade was getting steeper. He could hear the others clambering over the rocks behind him. They were getting closer.

And then his heart leaped. In the distance, nestled among the rocks, he saw a boat. Not much larger than a dinghy, but it looked seaworthy. If he could get to it, get it into the water, he might have a chance. The sun would be up soon. The shogun would not want to risk being seen and his men had the recording devices in their possession; surely, he would not pursue one crazy samurai at the risk of all the others.

Renewed by hope, the man leaped forward, tripped, and pulled himself up again. Only fifty yards to go. He could taste the briny mist from the waves crashing below. Forty yards. He was desperate, and his desperation gave him wings. The voices behind him were fading. He leaped again.

The man screamed as his left foot jammed into a steam vent, twisted, and shattered his lower leg. In a matter of seconds, he was surrounded.

They pulled him from the hole and dragged him to the beach. The shogun had already been sent for. Years seemed to pass before he returned from the boat. The man despaired, knowing his mission had failed; he grieved for his wife and children. They would never know what had happened to him, never know how much he had wanted to see them again. His mistake would mean a lifetime of suffering for them.

The shogun examined the recording devices—the microphone, the camera—and nodded. He was a superstitious man, but not an uneducated one. The implications were obvious.

At a word from him, one of the larger samurai stepped up and unsheathed his sword. The prisoner's arms were held and he was shoved forward at the waist. He saw his executioner's feet, watched him take his stance, knew when the blade came up . . .

And felt nothing as his neck was severed.

Chapter One

Secretary of State Warden Knox Hill hated having to call an ambassador home. It caused a stir in the host country and put the diplomat in a snit. As he waited for the American ambassador to Japan to walk through his door, he thought about what he was going to say. This meeting hadn't been his idea; but the president had insisted and an ambitious man did not disappoint the head of his party.

The door opened and James Palmer—sixtyish, graying, and professorial—walked in. Palmer had been the ambassador to Japan for nearly a decade, even married a Japanese national, and was highly regarded as an expert on Asian-American relations. Still, it wasn't his job to decide what information got passed on to his superiors and what didn't. If he wanted to keep his job, he'd have to shape up.

Palmer dropped his briefcase on the floor.

"This better be good, Ward," he huffed. "Twenty-six hours on a plane—Christ! Thank God my wife was free. Maybe we can salvage a vacation out of this."

Hill nodded. "I know it was a long trip to make on the spur of the moment, Jim. Have a seat."

Palmer sat down and Hill's secretary handed him a cup of tea. Now that he'd made his dramatic entrance, he seemed in no hurry for the meeting to start. Hill's eyes narrowed as the man made small talk. His opinion? James Palmer was soft. Soft and smug and self-absorbed, just like most of the diplomatic corps. The State Department was full of men like Palmer, men whose idea of diplomacy was boring the other guy to death.

"Let me get right to the point," Hill said. "The president is very unhappy about these latest election results."

Palmer sniffed. "Japan's a sovereign nation, Ward. I don't have any say over who they elect to their parliament. Is there something specific that's bothering you?"

"This Tanaka character."

"Iguchi Tanaka? What about him?"

"He's an ultra-nationalist, for God's sake."

Hill grabbed the CIA report he'd received just seventy-two hours before and waved it in Palmer's face.

"Do you know what he's proposing? A remilitarization of Japan and removal of all U.S. troops from the Pacific—the *Pacific* mind you, not just Okinawa—by 2010." He opened the report and flipped through the pages.

"The closing of Japanese markets to American goods, the restoration of imperial power. No wonder we can't get a decent trade agreement going with these people!" Hill tossed the report across his desk and it fell to the floor.

"Why do we have to get this stuff from the spooks, Jim? You're supposed to be our eyes and ears over there. What's happening?"

Palmer pursed his lips. "The reason I haven't given you a report on Tanaka is because, frankly, I don't consider him much of a threat."

"Not much of a threat," Hill echoed.

"No. Being a member of the Diet is like being in the House of Representatives. The man's only one voice out of many. It's not his fault they're dumping goods on us."

Hill considered that. He'd argued the same point with the president yesterday afternoon. But he'd need more than that to satisfy the chief executive; the man was acting like war in the Pacific was imminent.

"Given what the Japanese economy's been through the last couple of years," Palmer continued, "and Japanese xenophobia, a man like that was bound to get a sympathetic hearing. You've lived there. You know what the people are like."

Hill nodded. His year in the attaché's office had shown him the Japanese distrust of outsiders up close.

Palmer's lips tightened. "Quite frankly, Ward, if you guys were really worried about our relations with the Japanese, you'd have done something about the situation on Guam already."

Hill frowned. He had his finger on the pulse of a dozen hot spots scattered over the globe. *Was* there a situation on Guam?

"Refresh my memory."

Palmer set his jaw. "Japanese girls are being kidnapped on the island—all of them the daughters of very prominent businessmen, I might add. Only one was ever found and she was dead: washed up on the beach. No clues as to how she got there."

"I remember now. I thought we agreed that the Guamanians were going to handle it."

"They haven't. The governor did a sweep of the island and came up empty-handed; since then he's washed his hands of it. The island gets most of its money from tourism—most of it Japanese. I'm sure he figures that if word got out, it'd be bad for business."

Hill tapped his pencil on the desk. "Well, you can hardly blame him. A few teenagers go missing? Maybe they're runaways."

"It's more than that. Something's happening to these girls and it's bad."

"What makes you say that?"

"Rumors mostly, but—"

Hill scoffed.

"I know, I know." The ambassador held up his hands. "I was skeptical, too. But things have happened recently to change my mind. Two weeks ago, a man approached the Japanese authorities with information about the kidnappings."

"What kind of information?"

"I'm not sure; they're pretty tight-lipped about it. My guess is the intelligence was mishandled and the people responsible don't want any fingers pointed at them. They demanded more evidence from the guy before they'd look into his charges."

"And . . . ?"

"They wired him up and told him to record everything he saw and heard. Nobody's seen him since."

Hill shrugged. "A kook."

"I don't think so. He was a well-respected bureaucrat with a wife and two kids. He had too much to lose to go off the deep end."

"So you think he met with some sort of foul play?"

"I'm certain of it."

Hill considered that. "You mentioned rumors. What sort of rumors are we talking about?"

"Torture, ritual sacrifice—bizarre stuff."

"To what end?"

"Nobody knows. And frankly, if Japanese intelligence hasn't come up with the answer, I don't think either of us is going to."

Hill pinched the bridge of his nose. "Well, there's always the Navy."

Palmer was shaking his head. "Already been tried. The commander at Marianas has let it be known that none of his men will be put on 'baby-sitting detail.' His words, not mine."

Hill shrugged. "I don't know what to tell you then, Jim. If the Guamanians won't help and the military's not interested, what can the State Department do?"

Palmer leaned forward. "You could point out to the president that finding those girls would be an important goodwill gesture to the Japanese government. Something that might be a good idea, considering the support Tanaka and his kind got in the election."

"I thought you said Tanaka wasn't a threat."

"He isn't—yet. But he's got the ear of the prime minister now, and the cabinet's got some openings coming up."

Hill sat back, feeling outmaneuvered. He'd called Palmer in because Tanaka was a threat; if he turned down Palmer's advice and Tanaka gained influence, he'd look bad. But Warden Hill wasn't any more convinced of Tanaka's strength than James Palmer was. He wasn't going to be bullied into anything.

"No. The president's worried about Iguchi Tanaka,

not the current regime; and once he gets his trade agreement, he'll stop worrying about Tanaka, too. Let the Japanese solve the problem on Guam themselves. We've got enough problems of our own to deal with."

The ambassador nodded stiffly. "All right; but let me know if you change your mind." He stood and shook Hill's hand. "I'll give my office a call and have them put together a file on Tanaka as soon as possible."

"Good. I'll be waiting for it."

Palmer turned to go.

"Jim?"

"Yes?"

"No more surprises, okay? The president went nuts when he got this report and I got my ass chewed. From now on, if something like this is on the horizon, give me a heads-up. It'll make life a whole lot easier for both of us." He grinned. "And it'll keep you from having to catch another red-eye to Washington."

When the door closed, Warden Hill pulled out the little tape recorder that he kept in the top drawer of his desk and began dictating his notes of the meeting. He kept thorough notes of every meeting he had, just in case. If any of his actions were questioned later, he wanted to have his backside covered.

The intercom buzzed.

"Yes?"

"Sorry to bother you, Mr. Secretary; but the ambassador's wife would like a word with you. She says it'll only take a minute."

The secretary sighed. No doubt this would be an invitation for him and his lovely wife to join the Palmers for dinner.

He took a deep breath. "Fine. Show her in."

The door opened just as he was shoving the tape recorder back into his desk. When he looked up, his heart caught in his throat.

It was Miki.

As the door closed behind her, she stepped forward and bowed deeply from the waist, her slim figure as lithe as the last time he'd seen her. He stood and bowed automatically in return.

"Mr. Secretary Hill," she said in her gently affected voice. Then more quietly: "Warden-san."

Warden Hill didn't know what to say. For a moment, he was transported back fifteen years to a tiny apartment in Yokohama with a breathtaking view of Mt. Fuji and a beautiful girl who had picked up the pieces of his broken heart and put them back together.

"How have you been?" he asked.

"I am well," she said, inclining her head.

"You look well," he said. "I mean, you look terrific." He felt like a schoolboy, tripping over his own tongue.

Miki blushed. "You are too kind."

"No. No, I'm just being honest." He motioned toward the chair. "Please. Have a seat."

Miki stepped around the chair and sat down, folding her hands in her lap. Hill couldn't stop looking at her. The long black hair that she used to brush every morning in front of the mirror had a few strands of silver in it now and the face was showing signs of age; but she was, if anything, even more beautiful than he remembered.

"I missed you," he said, taking his seat behind the desk.

"I missed you, too, Warden-san."

"I never wrote."

"It was not expected."

Warden Hill swallowed, suddenly ashamed of the way he'd treated Miki. After living with her for a year, he'd dumped her and the life they'd made for . . . what? A big office on the Potomac and a house in Georgetown? Seemed like a pretty wretched trade-off.

"How is your wife?"

"She's fine." He nodded toward the door. "I see you're married to the ambassador now."

Miki smiled wistfully. "Yes. James and I met shortly after his first wife passed away. We have been married almost seven years."

"Are you happy?"

She hesitated and her words were spoken carefully. "James is . . . very kind."

Hill sat back and tried to get a grip. They weren't

here to rehash the past; she'd come to ask him to a reception or something. Might as well get it over with and let her go.

"Look, Miki, if you've come about a party—"

"No. Not that."

"Well, whatever it is, Jane and I aren't going to be able to make it."

Miki looked at her hands. "I have not come to ask you to dinner. I have come to ask you for a favor."

Warden Hill was taken aback. "What kind of favor?"

"I would like you to help find the girls who were kidnapped on Guam."

"Look, I already told Jim—"

"Two more girls were taken last week, Warden-san. One of them was my brother's daughter, Aiyako."

"God, I'm sorry. Really I am. But I just don't know what—"

"Aiyako is an only child," Miki said. "She is her parents' . . . how do you say? Pride and joy."

"Yes. Pride and joy."

Miki took a deep breath and Warden noticed that her hands were shaking. He frowned.

"No one outside my family know that Aiyako is not my brother's child. She is . . . adopted. Her mother had no husband, you see, and my brother and his wife had no children of their own."

"I'm sorry, but I don't see—"

"Warden, please. You must help us find Aiyako. She is only a girl. Who knows what will happen to her?"

"But Miki, why me? This is a domestic problem. Your people should be handling it."

Miki licked her lips and grew very still. When she looked up, there were tears in her eyes.

"Aiyako," she said softly. "Aiyako is . . . your child, Warden-san."

Hill fell back in his chair. "Why didn't you tell me?"

"You were gone and I know your father did not approve of me. My brother and his wife wanted the baby. I was happy to make them happy."

He nodded numbly, stood, then walked to the window. "Does Jim know?"

"No one know. Only my brother and his wife."

"What's she like?"

"Aiyako is very pretty girl—tall for Japanese. No one know her blood is mix. She is fourteen now and very smart. You can be proud."

Warden Hill bit his knuckle angrily. "So why tell me now? To make me feel guilty?"

"No, no! Only because she need your help," she said. "Japanese government will not admit its mistake and the governor of Guam will not help us. My only hope is you, Warden-san."

Warden Hill felt sick. He put his hands in his pockets and stared out at the Potomac. Fifteen years ago, he'd let his father persuade him to leave his post as attaché to the Japanese mission and return to the family's law firm. He had more money and more power now than most men in the history of the world. But what did any of it mean if he couldn't use it to help his own child?

The president would want to know why, of course. Warden could tell him what the ambassador had suggested—that it was a goodwill gesture to a friendly government under pressure from within. Tanaka's threat could be a useful excuse, under the circumstances.

But how, exactly, could the United States help? The president couldn't mobilize American troops just to find one girl. And the Guamanian governor would be furious if he found out the CIA was working operatives on the island without notifying him.

It would take a special type of operation to infiltrate the kidnappers and save Aiyako. One that could ferret out the perpetrators without being detected and bring them to justice without straining U.S.–Guamanian relations. And there was only one group Warden Hill knew of that fit that description.

He turned away from the window and nodded.

"All right, Miki. I'll see what I can do."

Chapter Two

Dr. Sarah Greene stepped out into the balmy Atlanta evening and looked around. Palmetto bugs skittered along the sidewalk and fireflies congregated under the magnolia trees, blinking and bobbing like flares on the ocean. Behind her, the imposing facade of the Centers for Disease Control jutted upward like the prow of a ship. She locked the door behind her and headed for the car. This time tomorrow, she'd be back in Cambridge, doing research in some stuffy basement library; but tonight she was on top of the world.

Sarah had taken the summer off from her post-doc studies at MIT to work out the bugs in the new antiviral drug she'd developed at the Centers for Disease Control. The compound—still known only by its laboratory designation, AV–22–12—had been devastatingly effective in laboratory trials and there were hopes that it would replace the antiviral "cocktails" that were currently being used in the fight against AIDS. But the first human trials had been only marginally successful, and Sarah Greene wasn't used to being a "marginal" success. When her old boss, John Thompson, called and told her there was a problem, she'd caught the first plane back to Atlanta.

Coming back had been tough. Sarah was no one's idea of a Southern belle. A snowboarder, she was as wild and crazy off the slopes as she was on them. The other researchers parted in front of her like the Red Sea as she walked the halls with her spiky black hair, baggy shorts, and a name tag on her lab coat that said: "That's DOCTOR Asshole to you!"

Still, Sarah had been disappointed the day she told John she was leaving.

"Sure," he'd said. "If that's what you want."

Like all the work she'd done for him had been nothing but ordinary. Well, tonight she'd solved the mystery that John and his crew of lab rats hadn't been able to crack in a year. As she stepped off the curb and headed across the parking lot, Sarah was feeling good. So good, in fact, that she didn't notice she was being followed.

They loomed out of the shadows and stepped quickly across the parking lot behind her. Sarah was halfway to the car when she heard them.

Footsteps. Coming up from behind. Getting closer.

She took a deep breath and squelched the urge to run. This was probably nothing; but if it was, running would only speed things up. She needed time to think.

Thirty yards from the car, the footsteps sped up. There was no denying it; someone was after her. Sarah closed her eyes and felt herself go very still. She dropped her backpack and turned.

There were two of them. One big, one small. One white, one black. Dressed in hooded sweatshirts and baggy jeans.

The black one flashed an uncertain smile. "Hey pretty lady. How you doing tonight?"

His partner smirked. "That ain't no lady. Look at that hair."

The two of them guffawed.

Sarah was in no mood for small talk. "What are you doing here?"

The men glanced at each other and grinned.

"We just lookin' for some fun." The shorter man turned and addressed the hulk beside him. "Don't she look like fun to you?"

"Oh yeah," he leered. "She look like a lot of fun to me."

Sarah's eyes narrowed. Adrenaline pumped through her veins as she weighed her options. The big guy was a good foot taller than she was—six four, maybe six five—but he looked soft. It was the little one who'd be the problem. Take him out and the big guy would lose heart.

"Leave now and I won't call the cops."

"The cops?" The little man sneered. "Lady, there ain't a cop around for miles. Go ahead. Scream your fuckin' head off."

Sarah carefully slipped out of her shoes and spread her feet. Gripping the asphalt with her toes, she crouched to maintain her balance and raised her arms. The two men looked at her with growing amusement.

"What's that? Some kinda Kung Fu pose?" The shorter man pointed and laughed. "Can you believe this?"

Sarah shook her head. "I'm telling you, you're making a big mistake."

"The only mistake we makin' is standin' here listenin' to you. Now, we can do this the easy way or we can do it the hard way. It don't make no difference to me."

"Have it your way then."

The small man nodded and the big man lunged. Sarah pivoted, deftly moving out of reach. The man staggered, regained his balance, and lunged again. Once again, Sarah stayed just out of reach.

"We haven't got all night," his accomplice yelled. "Grab her!"

The hulk charged a third time, but this time Sarah ducked, going down on one knee. As the big man cried out in astonishment, she cut his legs out from under him and flipped him over her back. He landed on the ground with a thud.

Sarah turned and looked at the little man. "My offer still stands. Leave now and I won't turn you in."

The shorter man's eyes narrowed. "Forget it lady. I'd been thinkin' I might leave you in one piece; but this is personal now."

He reached for his belt and Sarah saw a flash of metal.

No time to think. Sarah took two steps and kicked, her right heel slamming into the man's chest. He fell back and sprawled on the ground.

"What the—"

Placing her foot on his chest, Sarah pulled out the tire iron he'd jammed down the leg of his pants.

"You won't be needing this anymore," she said, throwing it into the bushes.

Then Sarah heard something behind her. The big man was on his feet, charging her from behind. She curled into a ball and thrust backward into his knees. This time, though, he was ready. She only succeeded in knocking him off balance. The little man was on his feet now, too. Sarah's breath came quick and hard as they circled her like wolves. She stood still, waiting for them to make the first move.

When it came, it was amateurish.

The big man charged head on, the little man from behind. Sarah feinted left. The big man raised his arm and brought it down. Sarah deflected it with her left forearm and struck out with her right palm. The heel of her hand caught the man under his chin and snapped his head back. Sarah completed the turn and struck out behind her with her left foot.

And hit nothing but air.

Seeing his partner go down, the little man had stopped just short of Sarah's strike zone. Sarah sneaked a quick look at the man on the ground. He wouldn't be getting up any time soon. She turned and looked at the remaining aggressor.

"Still want to have fun with me?"

He hesitated, his eyes glued to the behemoth on the ground, then slowly shook his head.

"Who are you?"

Sarah smirked. "I'm your worst nightmare, punk. Now beat it."

He didn't have to be told twice.

As the little man disappeared into the shadows, Sarah stepped over to the man on the ground and did a quick check of his vital signs. Respiration was normal—no blockage of the airways. Pulse was strong, if rapid. She took out her keys and checked his pupillary response with the tiny flashlight she used as a key fob. Everything normal. When he woke up, he'd have a headache and that neck would be stiff for a few days, but he'd live. Sarah stood up and dusted herself off.

The shrill sound of a pager cut through the still night air. Sarah glanced at her backpack and shook her head. This would be John, wanting to know if she'd made any progress. Why couldn't she just turn the damned pager off when she left the office, like other people? It was getting to be a pain. She popped open the lid and checked the message. It wasn't John.

It was Sam.

Sarah swallowed, her heart beating faster as the rest of the message scrolled past.

They needed her in Washington right away. The team had a job to do.

Chapter Three

They met in a windowless box surrounded on all sides by six feet of reinforced concrete. The rest of the team was already there when Sarah arrived. Travis returned her salute and Jack gave her a soul-brother handshake, but the rest merely nodded as she walked toward her seat. It was always awkward when they hadn't seen each other in a while. Where else in the world could any one of them walk into a room and find his or her equal, much less six of them? She sat down in her place at the long mahogany table and glanced around at the rest of the big guns.

At the head of the table was the leader of the group, Travis Barrett, a Green Beret who by all accounts had been born with a buzz cut. This morning, he was in his trademark GI Joe outfit: green T, camo pants, dog tags and boondockers. Sarah hadn't liked Travis the first time they met. She'd had him pegged as an obnoxious, overbearing, woman-hating putz with a testosterone problem; but now she knew better. He liked women just fine.

Next to Travis was Stan Powczuk, the team's second in command and Sarah's least favorite. Stan was a little guy by the team's standards—he said he was five foot nine—and he had a typical short-guy attitude. Quick to anger, slow to cool, always looking for a slight where none was intended. And always out to prove himself. Even with a wife at home, he'd schtup anything in a skirt. Too bad for him his wife, Angela, could sniff out

infidelity like a terrier looking for rats. After his last
indiscretion, she'd dropped a bowling ball out their
second-story window onto the hood of Stan's new Cor-
vette and almost sent Stan out after it. Knowing he had
Angela at home to deal with almost made Sarah feel
sorry for Stan.

Almost.

Jennifer Olsen was sitting on the other side of Stan.
As Sarah glanced at her, Jen looked up and winked. It
was funny. You'd think two women on a team like this
would have a tough time getting along, but Sarah and
Jen were like two peas in a pod. Two very different peas,
granted, but peas with a mutual respect and affection for
one another. Sarah smiled back, wondering what it must
be like to look like Jennifer Olsen. The woman could
give Barbie an inferiority complex. Walking down the
street together, the two of them were a study in con-
trasts—the Amazon and the waif from Woodstock.

Hunter Evans Blake the Third was on the other side
of Jen, the two of them looking like the bride and groom
on top of a wedding cake. Hunter was a little too
GQ-pretty boy for Sarah; but he was one hot-shit pilot
and he'd gotten her ass out of enough slings that she'd
developed something of a crush on him. Not that she'd
ever do anything about it. Hunter went through women
like a wildfire through tinder. Besides, who wanted to
date a guy who was better looking than you were? She
might wonder what it would be like to run her hands
over those rippling abs, but the heartache hangover
wouldn't be worth it.

The last two members—Jacques DuBois and Sam
Wong—sat on Sarah's right. Jacques, who everyone called
Jack, looked like a recruiting poster for the Marines;
rumor had that under his dusky skin his blood ran red,
white, and blue. He was abrasive in a big-city kind of way,
but he'd had a tough childhood, and it had given his abra-
siveness an odd kind of vulnerability—a combination that
was better than all the aphrodisiacs in the world.

Sam Wong, on the other hand, was nothing *but* vulner-
abilities. The first time Sarah met him, she wondered if
he'd wandered into the wrong room. Short and stringy,

with nerdy glasses that made his eyes look like they were set in the back of his head, he'd evoked a real sense of pity from Sarah until he opened his mouth.

"Enough beef in here to start a cattle ranch," he'd muttered as he took his seat.

By Sarah's estimation, Sam's intellect was the only one of the group's that came close to hers. And he had a wicked sense of humor, too, which he used to great effect against anyone who underestimated him.

The door opened and TALON's commander, Brigadier General Jack Krauss, walked in. Krauss was the head of the Joint Task Force and his orders officially came from the Chairman of the Joint Chiefs of Staff, General George H. Gates, via CINC SOCOM General Samuel Freedman; but in truth, the CIA, the NSA, and the State Department all had access to TALON's talents if the need arose.

Krauss set his briefcase on the table and welcomed everyone warmly. Even though he was of flag rank, Krauss refused to indulge in the kind of pomp and circumstance that gave most of the higher-ups a hard-on. Whenever TALON had a mission, Krauss would show up, give them their assignment, and leave them to work out the details. Sarah knew she wasn't the only one who appreciated his no-bull attitude.

It was Krauss who'd appointed Travis Barrett the group's leader. Since there were no ranks in the Force, they needed a top dog to give them some cohesion, keep them from running off in seven different directions trying to save the world. Sarah suspected that each one of them thought he or she was superior to all the others; but you had to think that way if you were going to be a member of TALON Force. If you didn't, you'd never survive.

As the team members watched, General Krauss booted up the computer and inserted a disk into the CD-ROM drive. Sam had everything all set up; once the disk was cued, the show would begin.

The lights dimmed and the first page of the report lit up the screen.

Technologically Augmented Low-Observable, Networked Force
TALON Force.

Sarah felt the same adrenaline rush she'd felt the first time she read that acronym—sitting in this room, in the dark, with the others. TALON was an elite group of men and women whose sole purpose was to conduct covert ops in support of American interests anywhere and everywhere those interests were threatened. Sarah had an M.D. from Johns Hopkins, a black belt in Kung Fu, and a snowboard rip that had qualified her for the Olympics. But nothing—nothing—meant as much to her as being part of TALON Force.

The next page came up and Krauss began his spiel.

"In the past three months, ten girls—all of them Japanese nationals—have disappeared from the island of Guam while on vacation with their families. Only one of them has ever been recovered."

The slide changed and Sarah leaned forward to get a better look. It was a standard autopsy photo, a frontal view of the head and thorax. The eye sockets were ragged and empty, the flesh of the face bloated and pockmarked. The rest of the torso was similarly ravaged, the rib cage bare where the left breast had been torn away.

"Toxicology reports?" she asked.

Krauss glanced at her. "Liver analysis positive for alcohol and morphine."

"She OD'd?"

"No. Death was due to drowning." He indicated the picture on the screen. "What you see is the result of scavenging by the local fauna."

Sarah nodded and sat back as Krauss continued.

"At the behest of the Japanese government, the governor of Guam ordered a sweep of the island last month and came up empty-handed. Wherever the girls are, they're no longer on Guam."

Travis turned. "General," he began in his Texas drawl, "when you say 'searched,' are you talkin' about a house-to-house?"

Krauss nodded. "For the most part. Hotels and other

temporary housing units were monitored by management. I think we can assume they were pretty thorough."

"What about houseboats, yachts, junkers anchored in the bay?"

"All searched. Except for this one, none of the girls has ever turned up."

Jen frowned. "So they were kidnapped. The question is, why?"

"That's easy," Stan barked. "Prostitution's big in Southeast Asia. Some pimp just found a new supply to tap into, that's all."

Sarah shook her head. "That doesn't make sense, Stan. Pimps look for girls who won't be missed. Why not take some street urchin?" She looked back at Krauss. "Unless this one was the exception . . . ?"

"Glad you asked." He pressed the controller in his hand and the slide changed. "We had our analysts put everything we knew about the girls into the computer to see if there were any correlations. I think you'll agree there are some startling similarities."

There were. According to the slide, the girls were all between the ages of twelve and sixteen, all enrolled at exclusive private schools in Japan, all from traditional families, all the daughters of prominent and influential businessmen, and all in the company of a chaperon at the time they were abducted.

Sam pointed. "What about the time frame? Was there any pattern to when they were taken?"

Another slide.

"The abductions occurred in clusters," Krauss said.

"Correlating to what?"

"We don't know."

Travis looked at Sam.

"Think you could take a look at the data and come up with something?"

"That's just what I was thinking."

Krauss nodded. "I'll get it to you as soon as we finish here."

The slide changed again. This time it was of a sweet-faced Japanese girl in a blue kimono.

"The last girl taken was the niece of the American ambassador to Japan."

"She looks so young," Jennifer said.

"They're all young; and they need to be found—now. However—and this is important—under no circumstances are the civilian authorities on Guam to know you're there. Relations with the governor would be severely strained if he found out we were working operatives on the island without his knowledge."

"So some girls are missing," Hunter said. "What's TALON supposed to do about it?"

Krauss set his mouth. "You may not be aware of it, Captain Blake, but U.S.–Japanese relations are at an all-time low. We need to turn the tide and the president has decided that this is the way to do it.

"Find the girls," Krauss said simply. He switched off the computer and the lights came up. "And find out who's taking them and why."

Sarah looked at the others. No one said anything, but there were skeptical looks all around.

"Here are your orders." Krauss handed the file to Travis. "The president wants to see some progress on this as soon as possible. If our estimates are correct, the kidnappers will be looking for more victims in about a week." He glanced at Sam. "Maybe sooner, if Mr. Wong finds something we didn't."

He picked up his briefcase. "Good luck, team. Your country is counting on you."

Chapter Four

The door had barely shut behind Krauss when all hell broke loose.

"What kind of assignment is this?" Stan barked. "Find some missing girls? *Fuck* that!"

"I hate to say it," Sarah said, "but I agree with Stan. Missing persons is cop stuff."

"Yeah," Jack agreed. "That shit is strictly Barney Fife."

"I don't know," Jen said thoughtfully. "General Gates wouldn't give us an assignment if he didn't think we were the only ones who could handle it. There must be something more to this than Krauss told us." She looked at Travis. "What's the story?"

Travis frowned as he flipped through the orders Krauss had given him.

"It says here the Secretary of State personally requested that TALON Force be detailed to this problem as a goodwill gesture to the Japanese government."

"Goodwill?" Hunter sounded incredulous. "Since when does TALON do charity work?"

Travis shook his head. "Sam? You're our Asian expert. What's going on over there?"

Sam pushed his glasses up and folded his hands on the table.

"Like Krauss said, things are tense. Trade negotiations have been stalled for almost a year and there's talk of an embargo; the latest elections were seen as a vote of no confidence in the ruling party; and Iguchi Tanaka's election is causing a big flap in the Diet."

"Tanaka? What's his drum?"

"Nationalism. Think Miloscvic with international clout. They just passed laws returning their pre-war national anthem and flag. Remember the Rising Sun?"

"Oh, for God's sake," Stan snorted. "The Japs are our friends. The war's over."

Sam's eyes narrowed. "Maybe so. But we Chinese remember the last time Japanese nationalism took hold." He glanced around the table. "Shiro Ishii made Joseph Mengele look like an angel of mercy. Tens of thousands of Chinese died in his germ warfare experiments. Maybe you numbskulls don't, but when I see signs of Japanese nationalism on the rise, I pay attention."

Travis held up his hands. "Whoa! Okay, Sam. We got your point."

"Yeah," Stan said. "What are you so hot about?"

Sam glanced at the table. "My mother's people are from Nanking."

There was an awkward silence as Travis flipped through the report.

"It says here that the police on Guam can't find the girls and the Navy won't help."

"Smart guys," Stan huffed.

There were nods all around.

Travis frowned. "It also says a good soldier doesn't question orders."

"Shit," Jack muttered. "Nobody said we wouldn't do it."

"It just seems like a waste of our talents," Sarah said.

"That's not for us to decide," Travis said mildly, his eyes still scanning the pages. He looked up. "Is it?"

They shook their heads. "No."

"Okay, then let's get to it. We've got a lot of work ahead of us." Travis handed the first few pages to Sam. "Scan these in; I want everyone to see this. Sarah, while he's doing that, take a look at this autopsy report and see what you can make of it."

Sarah took the bound pages and started reading.

A few minutes later, the slides were ready and the group began reviewing the data.

"Okay, first thing," Travis said. "What do we know about Guam?"

"It's an American protectorate," Jen said, "with a governor and a legislature, just like a state in the union."

"What else?"

"It saw some of the worst fighting during World War Two," Jack said. "The Japs were dug in all along the Marianas; flushing them out was a bloody job."

"It's volcanic," Sarah added, still reviewing the autopsy notes.

"It's an island," Stan said. "No way to get there except air and sea. The South Pacific's a motherfucker, too; lots of shipwrecks around there. Sharks, if you get in deep enough."

"Okay, so we're going to be dealing with tropical terrain: rain forest, sand, maybe volcanic rock and ash. When we finish here, I'll call Maui and have them get the course ready for us.

"Sarah, what does the autopsy tell us that might be helpful?"

Sarah put down the report. "Lungs full of salt water—cause of death was definitely drowning."

"What about the drugs?"

"Opiates and alcohol. My guess is she fell in the water and was too doped up to swim—assuming she knew how."

"Was she an addict?"

"Unlikely. No sign of cirrhosis on the liver biopsy, no tracks on the arms. Looks like the drugs were ingested, too—liquid morphine in a creme de menthe suspension. Whoever gave it to her wanted her alive—at least for a while."

"So how'd she get into the water?"

"Good question. Presumably, the kidnapper was trying to take her off the island."

"Her face sure looked bad," Jack said.

"Yeah," Sarah said. "Dead bodies are like sponges when they sit in the water; they swell up until the skin splits open. Crabs and seagulls probably picked out her eyes. Soft stuff goes fast; and in the tropics, the whole process speeds up. The coroner's report says she'd been dead about two days before they found her."

"And they found her a week after she'd been taken."

She nodded at Travis. "That's right."

"So, the kidnappers must have kept her somewhere on the island before dumping her into the water."

"I don't think they dumped her."

"Why not?"

"She had rope burns on her wrists. She'd been tied up before she fell into that water; I think she escaped, fell in, and drowned when she couldn't swim."

Travis considered that for a moment. "Okay. If these guys are taking the girls off the island, they must be bivouacked somewhere. Jack, when we get there I want you to recon the area, find out who might have seen them. Start at the waterfront and backtrack into the areas where the girls were abducted. I'll get you a map. Hunter, you take the airport. See who's taking what craft out. See if there are any private strips these guys could be using, too.

"Stan? You'll need to get us a boat. Try your contacts at the naval base first; if you can't get one without tipping your hand, see what the private sector's got. Tell 'em we need something big and fast, but with some range to it. If we have to chase these guys, I don't want to be out muscled. As soon as you secure the boat, give Jack a hand. We've got a lot of ground to cover and not much time."

Travis pointed at the screen with his laser pen. "It looks like the kidnappers are pretty darned sure they won't get caught. Their victims' families are raising Cain back home, the governor's ordered a sweep of the island, and so far they're still taking girls off the streets in broad daylight."

"Someone on the island must be helping them," Stan said.

Travis nodded. "I suspect you're right. But who? Jen, you're friendly with the spooks. See if you can get some intel on any local agitators. What kind of politics are going on down there? And why take only Japanese girls?

Why not Americans or French or Germans? Find out if anybody's got a grudge against Japan and if so, why."

"You got it."

"Next item." Travis glanced at Sam. "What is it about young girls that might be significant?"

Sam knit his brows thoughtfully. "Man, you've got a real mix of cultures on Guam; but young girls always mean innocence. Hindus, Buddhists, Muslims, and Shintos all have rituals and taboos regarding women."

"But they're not women," Jen corrected. "They're just kids."

Sam shrugged. "Lots of Eastern religions attribute magical powers to virgins. That's the only connection I can see."

Travis frowned. "You think this might be the work of a cult?"

"Maybe a cult to you; but to these people, their religion."

"So, how do we find them? If they *are* taking girls as part of a religious thing, they're not going to go around advertising it."

Stan scoffed. "You can't keep a thing like that quiet. Even the locals would have stumbled over them by now. This religion stuff's a red herring."

"Maybe so," Travis said. "But we still need to check it out. Remember what Krauss said? We've got to find the girls they've already taken, *and* stop them from doing it again. To do that, we've got to get right into the heart of whatever organization is doing this. Sam, once Jen gets her report from the spooks, the two of you put your heads together and come up with an intel estimate on potential threats."

"Will do."

"Once we know who they are, how do we find them?" Hunter asked.

"That's easy," Travis said. "We find some nice young Japanese girl, walk her around the streets until somebody takes her, and then see where they go."

Stan laughed. "Yeah, right. And where are we going to find a nice young girl like that?"

It only took a moment. Slowly, everyone turned to look at Sarah.

"Ohhhhhh no! Nuh-uh. Not me. I'm not going to be the bait. Forget it. Besides, I'm not Japanese. Look at me! You think nobody's going to notice these green eyes?"

"Brown contacts," Jen said.

"But my hair! No. I'm telling you, it won't work."

Travis looked at Jen. "Think you can do it?"

"Puh-leeze. A piece of cake. She's tiny; and the make-up's a cinch—"

"I don't want you puttin' any of your schmutz on my face!"

"I can teach her a few Japanese phrases," Sam offered.

Jen smiled pleasantly. "And when we get there, I can pose as her chaperon."

Sarah shook her head. "I'm telling you, it won't work. Come on, Trav, I don't want to be a sitting duck. Put me somewhere I can kick ass and take names."

"Maybe she's right," Stan said with a smirk. "I don't think even Jen could make her look like a girl."

Before Sarah could think of a caustic retort, Travis was talking again.

"All right. We've got a plan." He turned to Sam. "How soon can you tell us when the next girl will be taken?"

Sam shrugged. "Give me a day to run some analyses, I'll see what I can come up with."

"All right; if you don't come up with something better, we'll use Krauss's estimate of a week and hope that's soon enough." Travis ran a hand over his buzz cut. "Shit. That's going to cut our prep time down to nothing. Hunter? How fast can you get us to Guam from Maui?"

"Military or civilian aircraft?"

"Better make it a civvy. We don't want to draw attention to ourselves."

"I'll get a Lear. File the flight plan. We can be there in half a day."

Travis nodded. "Okay. You, Stan, Jack, and I will head to Maui tomorrow and spend a couple of days on maneuvers. There's still a possibility the girls are being held somewhere in the interior on Guam; I figure a day on the range, another on watercraft boarding, maybe a glass house drill, we'll be ready."

"What about us?" Jennifer said. "I'll need at least a day and a half in the studio to make a disguise for Sarah, and Sam's going to have to put together some words and phrases for her to learn. You don't need muscles for what we're going to do."

"You're right," Travis said. "Your time would be better spent turning our little tomboy into a geisha."

Sarah scowled.

"Sarah? We've got to assume the dead girl was drugged on purpose. Can you put together an antidote in two days?"

"Standard antidote for opiates is Naloxone. I can get it at Bethesda before I go."

"Good. And get enough for the others, too. We don't know what kind of shape they'll be in when we find them."

"Got it."

"You and Jen catch a commercial flight and meet us in Guam in three days. Sam, put together a list of the gear you're going to need for this operation. Anything we can't get on Maui, we'll have to take with us. We'll pick you up in the morning on our way out. Sound good?"

"Works for me."

"All right then. Let's go."

Chapter Five

August 18, 1806 hours local time (Zulu minus ten),
TALON Force secret training facility, Maui,
Hawaiian Islands

It was almost dusk. The moon going down in the west
was a thin slice of cool light that hung like a scimitar
over the banyan trees. Deep in the shadows, Travis Barrett lay on his belly, his brilliant suit blending flawlessly
into the jungle terrain as he watched the house. Still no
movement inside. He checked his watch, cupping his
hand around the luminous face to shield the glare:
1806 hours.

Thirty-six minutes ago, the TALON team members
had stepped out of their Combat Rubber Raiding Craft
and onto the beach in search of five civilians and an
unknown number of tangos holding them hostage. It had
taken twenty-nine minutes of chopping through heavy
jungle understory, some of it in knee-deep swamp water,
to acquire the target; now Jack was doing the initial
recon. While Stan and Hunter prepared to make an entrance, Travis kept an eye on the house. So far, no one
inside had made so much as a peep. Either no one was
at home, or the unfriendlies were damned sure no one
could get close without their knowing about it.

Jack was hunkered at Travis's right, watching the
readout from his Micro-UAV. A pilotless micro-aircraft,
the Unmanned Aerial Vehicle was a palm-sized delta
wing carrying a microelectronics payload that sent visual
data back to its user. Its low altitude and thirty-minute
flight time made it perfect for this kind of close-quarters

surveillance, and the quiet humming of its battery-powered rear-mounted pusher propeller was virtually undetectable in the field.

Jack was picking up the UAV's transmission on his Battle Sensor Device, or BSD, a monoclelike laser pathway that painted 3-D images onto his retina. As the data streamed in, he scowled in concentration.

"What is it?" Travis whispered.

"Simple construction: one door each, front and back, two windows, I'd say two, maybe three, bedrooms. They must be expecting us, though—the shades are down." He flipped up the monocle and recalled the UAV. The little aircraft made a beeline toward them and Jack plucked it effortlessly from the air. "We won't know the rest till we get inside."

Travis looked back at the house and checked the range finder on his BSD. Fifty meters to go. His brain was clicking a million miles an hour. Were the hostages still inside? If so, where were they? Together in one room or dispersed throughout the house? Were they injured or would they be able to walk out under their own power? And how many tangos were guarding them?

The perimeter had been checked and rechecked. Time to move in. Travis fingered the implant behind his right ear and whispered.

"Stan, you got your flash-bang ready?"

In his earpiece, Stan's hoarse whisper came through loud and clear. "Ready."

"Roger that. I think it's time to say hello. Jack, you go left, I'll take right. Once Stan throws the grenade, Hunter, you lead the charge. We'll go in on my signal."

Travis raised up on one elbow, squinting at the house again. Something just wasn't right. No one took hostages and then waited like sitting ducks. The sensors said he was fine, but his gut told him there was something he'd overlooked.

When in doubt, Travis listened to his gut.

He flipped up the BSD and scanned the ground in front of him, letting his knowledge of the terrain compensate for the low light. The way he figured it, all the hi-tech gadgetry in the world couldn't beat 20/10 vision.

There it was.

A trip wire, not more than three feet in front of him. Crude, but effective. One more step and he'd have given them all away.

Travis grinned and pointed it out to Jack. "Almost rang the doorbell," he whispered. "Stan, Hunter, you see this?"

Travis hunched himself into a squat and indicated the spot where the booby trap lay.

"Got it."

"Okay. Make sure you give it a wide berth when you come through."

"Will do."

Travis raised his fist to shoulder level and motioned his team forward. One by one, the rest of them stepped carefully over the wire and fanned out, crossing the fifty-meter distance in seconds.

Travis pressed his back against the right wall of the structure, his M-16 in his hands. Jack took his position on the other side of the door, also with an M-16. Hunter was holding one of the team's new XM-29 Smart Rifles, a nine pound 4.55mm weapon that used millimeter wave-directed smart bullets that would help keep him from taking out a hostage. Stan had an M-16 slung over his shoulder and a concussion grenade in his hand. At Travis's signal, Hunter raised the XM-29 to his shoulder. Stan kicked in the door and tossed his grenade.

There was a blinding flash and in the same instant an explosion. A cloud of white smoke poured out of the front door. Hunter charged inside.

"Go! Go! Go!"

The other three jumped through the door in rapid succession.

Travis swung his rifle around, crouching just inside the doorway. The only light came from a bare bulb in the kitchen. The BSD's thermal viewer allowed him to scan the room through the rapidly dispersing haze. He heard the *Pfft! Pfft!* of the XM-29 and saw a tango on his left go down. The room smelled of spent propellant and lead.

There was a hallway straight ahead that led into the back of the house. Hunter and Stan stood in front of

the wall to the left. With Hunter covering him, Stan
reached into his pack, pulled out a small saw and cut a
mouse hole in the wall leading to the first bedroom. The
entrance to the hallway was too tempting a place to put
a booby trap; going through a wall was nearly as fast
and far safer. Hunter stepped through with Stan close
on his heels and Travis heard another burst of fire.

Travis motioned to Jack, who ran right and cleared
another bad guy from the kitchen before returning to
cover the rear. Travis scuttled forward, stepped through
the mouse hole, and checked the room, looking in the
closet and under the bed for any hostages. Hunter and
Stan had already mouse-holed out the other side when
Jack stepped in from the front room. Travis shook his
head—nobody there—and motioned toward the door.
The two of them crossed the hallway to the second bedroom. Empty. The hostages must all be in one room.
But where? Travis turned and saw Jack press himself
against the wall, inching toward the door, prepared to
make a run down the hallway. As he jumped through
the door, Travis saw flashes and heard a burst of gunfire.
Then everything was quiet.

"I found 'em." Stan's voice was an urgent whisper in
Travis's ear.

Travis nodded. "Are we all clear then?"

"Negative," Hunter replied. "Still have one more
room to check."

Travis's eyes swept the room. Was this room secure?
Yes. He looked across the hallway and caught Jack's
eye, motioned toward the front room. Had any bad guys
snuck in since their arrival? Travis led the way as the
two of them headed back out the way they'd come.

The place had become deadly still. In the quiet, Travis's ears seemed to stretch, searching for any sound that
might mean danger. There were wood chips and drywall
pieces on the ground where Stan had sawn his mouse
holes and the floor was littered with spent M-16 car-
tridges. The stuff crunched underfoot as Travis approached the first mouse hole.

Pfft! Pfft!

Travis froze. "Everything okay back there?"

"It is now. How's the front of the house?"

"Jack and I are checking it now," Travis whispered.

He nodded toward Jack, who covered him as he burst through the mouse hole, rolling across the room and behind the couch. At his signal, Jack followed. Suddenly, a tango reared up from the far corner of the room. Travis squeezed off three shots—a perfect Mozambique—and the bad guy went down.

Jack grinned and nodded his approval.

Travis thumbed his transmitter. "Clear!"

"Clear!" Hunter replied.

Slowly, the spring that had been Travis's body uncoiled. His heart was still pounding, but the adrenaline rush was beginning to fade.

"Stan? Where are our hostages?"

"Back room. Tied up in a closet."

"Are they all right?"

"As all right as five sacks of grain with happy faces painted on 'em ever get."

Travis chuckled. Every time they practiced a hostage rescue, the "hostages" varied. Anything about the size and weight of a human being would do. Sometimes they were crash dummies, sometimes sacks of grain or bags of dog food. The time they rescued a group of school children from a bus, the "kids" were a herd of goats.

The team stood in the front room, catching their breath, and looked around. The outside walls of the house were nothing more than two-by-four framing and Sheetrock, the floors bare dirt. The tangos had all been either pop-up dummies or posters of masked men holding guns; but in the heat of battle, none of that mattered. If you were good at what you did, you did your job and let your imagination provide the rest. TALON Force members were very good at what they did.

"All right," Travis said, examining the rescued grain sacks. "I think we're ready for D-Day." He stepped outside and called for a helo. When he was sure it was on its way, he took off his helmet and ran a hand over his buzz cut.

"Any of you boys feel like a drink?"

Chapter Six

The party was already underway when Travis walked into the bar. Wahini Lei's was a popular after-hours hangout on Maui. Hunter and Jack were at a table in the back, a pair of Heineken bottles in front of them. Stan was out on the floor, dancing with a local girl in a pink sarong who shimmied up and down his body while he stood in place doing the herky-jerky. The place was smoky and dark and the music blaring from the speakers over the bar felt like a jackhammer to the brain. Travis stepped up to the bar and waited to give his order. Forget the bottle babies; he wanted a draft. Something strong and dark to match his mood.

The communiqué had come through as he was leaving to join the others. Special intel from the spooks in Japan. Nobody was willing to say so on the record, but if the information was true, the team's mission had just taken an ominous turn.

"That boy a friend of yours?"

Travis turned, startled by the unmistakable twang of a fellow Texan, and did a quick recon of the woman who had spoken to him. Brunette, bedroom hair, big baby blues, and a pair of perky tits that pointed at him about chest level.

She indicated the specter of Stan, now doing his own version of dirty dancing with his lady love.

Travis nodded. "Yeah, I know him."

The woman raised an eyebrow. "Well, I'll say this for

him, he adds some real atmosphere to the place." She lifted her chin. "You want a drink or are you just holding up the bar?"

Travis smiled. "No, ma'am. I'm just waiting to place my order. You know, you are one tall drink of water."

"Yeah, we grow 'em big in Texas."

"I thought I recognized the accent. Where you hail from?"

"Fort Worth. What'll you have?"

"Gimme a Pau Hana Porter. What are you doing so far from home?"

She chuckled and turned her back on him. "Pau Hana Porter, coming right up."

As she grabbed a glass from under the counter, Travis leaned over the bar for a better view.

Nice legs, too.

She drew down the draft, gripping the handle with authority. Travis liked the way she looked, liked even better the way she talked. She had a smoky voice that seemed to ooze sex with every syllable.

"So, you boys going to be in town long?" she asked, setting his glass down on the bar.

"Nope. Leaving in the morning."

"Too bad."

"Yeah." Travis grinned, trying not to look at her chest. "I was hoping to maybe see some points of interest." He opened his wallet and took out a ten. "What's your name, anyway?"

"Maggie. What's yours?"

"Travis."

"Good name for a Texan."

"My parents thought so."

She reached into the till and he waved away the change.

"Keep it," he said. "It was worth it to hear a real American again."

She closed the till and smiled. "Y'all come back now, y'hear?"

"You can count on it."

He turned and took a swig of beer, then walked over to the table, his stomach churning.

"Hey, Boss," Jack said. "Where's Sam?"

"Back at the hotel playing with his toys."

Hunter nodded. "We were starting to think you got lost."

Travis set his drink down and pulled up a chair. "Nope. Just got a message from HQ, that's all. Had to hear 'em out before I left." He glanced at Stan and the Hawaiian girl, still out on the dance floor.

"Who's the BIQ?" The Bitch in Question.

"Stan's local squeeze. Picked her up on the way here."

"Jesus, how does he do it?"

Hunter curled his lip. "He's an asshole."

"Look who's talking," Jack laughed. "You've got—what—two, three fillies in your stable?"

"That's different. I'm not married to any of them. Stan promised to be faithful in front of God and everybody."

Travis grinned. "Hunter, I do believe you're showing your Puritan roots."

"Bullshit. It's one thing to go nuts after maneuvers; but stringing along a herd of pussy on the side's another."

"But if *you* string 'em along, it's okay? I'd like to hear you parse that one, professor."

Hunter leaned forward and smiled. "I never tell them I love them—ever. It's as simple as that. If they make more of the relationship than there is, that's their problem. My conscience is clear."

Travis smirked and Jack rolled his eyes.

"Well, thanks for clearing that up for us."

"So," Jack said, "what's the word from HQ? The show still a go?"

"Yeah," Travis said, his good mood evaporating. "But I want to get Stan in on this, too, before we talk about it." He stood up and motioned to Stan, who gave his sweetheart a sloppy French kiss and left her to boogie on her own for a while.

"Finally decided to join us, huh?" He picked up a chair and set it down next to Jack, the four of them forming a semicircle, backs to the wall. Even off duty, they just naturally assumed a defensive posture.

Travis nodded. "I was telling Jack and Hunter that I

got a message from HQ as I was walking out the door. It's about the mission. I think you three ought to hear about it before we get too drunk tonight."

"Did they come to their senses and call it off?"

Jack chuckled. "Yeah. Maybe they got the Boy Scouts to do it instead."

Hunter guffawed.

"Stow it," Travis growled.

"Come on, Trav. Finding a bunch of girls? That's junior league," said Stan. "TALON shouldn't even be involved."

"I don't care what it looks like to you dickheads," Travis said. "You don't know all the facts."

"Okay," Stan said, folding his arms. "Tell us the facts."

Travis took a deep breath.

"Turns out the Japanese government had an informant who said he knew something about the people who took the girls."

"They *had* an informant?"

"Yeah. He disappeared."

Stan shook his head. "Man, this is so lame."

Travis glowered. "He told them the girls were being used for ritual sacrifices by some religious fanatics—not your run-of-the-mill bad guys." He picked up his beer and rolled it between his palms. "They didn't believe him."

"Who would?" Hunter said. "It sounds like the guy was going a little heavy on the sake."

"I don't think so. Our people did a thorough background check on the guy—he was clean. Nice job, nice house, nice family, no police record, nothing."

"So?"

"So, he knew his story was crazy. Why risk all that if it wasn't true?"

The others shrugged.

"Here's what's bothering me. When we send Sarah out on the streets, she's not going to have her chameleon suit or her helmet or her weapon. And we still don't know if these people are on Guam or someplace else. We don't know what kind of terrain we're going to have to meet them on. We don't even know their capabilities yet."

Jack spoke. "As Sun Tzu said, 'When you are ignorant of the enemy but know yourself, your chances of winning are equal.'"

"Exactly; I don't like the odds."

They sat at the table in silence, locked in their own thoughts as the craziness carried on around them. No one said what Travis was thinking: that it had been his idea to hang Sarah out as bait. That it would be his fault if she got hurt.

"As far as I'm concerned," he continued, "this mission is as important as any other. I don't want anything to happen to Sarah because you assholes didn't take it seriously."

Stan shook his head. "Don't worry about me," he said. "I'll do my job."

"Yeah, me too," said Jack.

Hunter nodded. "You can count on me, Travis."

"Good. That's all I wanted to hear."

Stan slapped his hands on the table and stood. "Well, if that's all, I have a date on the dance floor."

"Sure, Stan," Travis said. "Go have fun."

The waitress came by and took their orders for another round. Travis glanced back at Maggie making drinks at the bar, caught her eye, and raised his glass in a toast. She put a hand on her hip, then shook her head and laughed at him. God, she was beautiful. Too bad she was working tonight.

Hunter looked at Jack. "Don't look now, but I think you've attracted some attention."

Travis picked up his beer and glanced in the same direction. "I believe he's right, Jack. Goddamn jarheads get all the girls."

Jack looked disgusted. "Don't tell me, let me guess. Tiny little thing? Head full of brown curls? Tight ass? Big eyes?"

"That's an affirmative."

"I thought so. She asked me to dance when we first got here. I'm not interested."

"Not interested?" Hunter said. "Why the hell not? Look at her. She's hot."

Jack shook his head. "No way. Scrawny little thing like that? I'd split her like firewood. Nuh-uhn. I need a woman with something I can hold on to. I ain't no baby fucker."

Hunter turned his head, trying not to laugh.

"Jack," Travis said, "you are the most considerate son of a bitch I've ever met. Won't screw a woman on principle. I'm amazed." He surveyed the room. "So, who *do* you have your eye on, big man?"

Jack nodded toward a table across the room. "See the blonde in the blue shorts? She and I have been on the same channel ever since I sat down here."

Hunter glanced over his shoulder. "Jesus, she's a big one. Travis, check out those legs. The woman's a human nutcracker."

Jack grinned. "What's the matter? Can't you white boys handle them thighs?"

Travis turned and eyed the woman, a voluptuous blonde in blue satin hot pants and a T-shirt she'd wedged a pair of D-cups into. As he watched, she glanced over at Jack and bit her lower lip.

"Holy shit, Jack. Go catch her before she slips off the chair!"

"No. Can't make my move yet."

"Why not? Jesus, the girl's begging for it."

"I'm waiting for her friend to leave." Jack indicated the cute redhead on the girl's right.

"Hell, if that's all that's stopping you . . ." Hunter stood up.

Jack looked at him. "What are you doing?"

"I'm taking care of the friend." Hunter grinned. "My pleasure."

Jack leaped up and the two of them crossed the room.

Travis shook his head and laughed, feeling the weight lifting from his shoulders. He'd said his piece and the rest of them had understood. In the morning, he'd give Jen and Sarah a call and let them know what was going on.

He glanced at the door—Stan was leaving. He glanced

toward the table—Jack and Hunter were leading their
girls out onto the dance floor. It looked like Travis could
finally let his own hair down a little, if one could let
down a buzz cut. He glanced at the bar and frowned.
No Maggie. Now where did that girl go?

A waitress came by and started picking up the empty
glasses. Travis asked her if she knew where Maggie
had gone.

"She left," she said casually. "Her shift was over at
ten."

"Oh." Travis looked down at the table, feeling foolish.
Maybe he'd been wrong. Maybe there was no chemistry
there after all. The waitress was still standing next to
him. Oh well. If he couldn't get laid, he might as well
get drunk.

"Get me a refill, will you? Looks like I'm going to be
here a while."

"Oh, I don't think so." She grinned at him. "I've got
something for you." She reached inside her blouse and
pulled out a folded piece of paper. "Here," she said.
She handed it to him and walked away.

What the hell . . . ?

It was a cocktail napkin. Travis unfolded it. There was
a note scribbled on the inside:

> *Tex,*
> *If you're still interested in those points of interest, meet*
> *me at my car in ten minutes. Red Dodge Ram pickup*
> *with a cab-over camper parked on the north side. If*
> *not, have a nice life.*
>
> *Maggie*

Travis grinned and let out a whoop. Looked like he
was going to score after all.

He grabbed his jacket and walked to the dance floor,
tossing the car keys to Jack. He figured Maggie could
give him a ride home. He headed out the door, whistling.

Chapter Seven

Jennifer was proud of the little studio she kept in West-
wood. Just a quick drive from Hollywood, it was as well-
equipped as any FX shop in the valley—maybe better,
since TALON Force gave her access to the latest technology from Washington. She'd spent a year learning
magic tricks in Vegas; but who needed magic when you
had stuff like this?

Still, transforming facial features believably was more
art than science—especially when that transformation involved the eyes. Eyelids had to be flexible enough for
the wearer to blink, yet firm enough to hold their shape.
As Jen sat at her workbench, feathering the edges of the
foam latex eye flaps that Sarah would wear on Guam,
she hoped that they'd be good enough to fool whoever
was taking those girls.

Jen had spent yesterday morning creating a plaster
cast of Sarah's face in preparation for making the latex
prosthetics. She'd started by making a mold of Sarah's
face using cold-set alginate, similar to the stuff dentists
used to model teeth. It was a delicate process, made
more so by the fact that even the sanest person can
become claustrophobic when their face is covered in rapidly solidifying goo. Jennifer had seen Stallone literally
claw the stuff from his face in panic; but Sarah was men-
tally tough. As Jennifer added the gauze strips to stabi-
lize the alginate, Sarah sat perfectly still, blowing
forcefully out her nostrils when the alginate threatened

to close them over and using self-hypnosis to remain
calm. Once the stuff was dry, all it took was a grimace
for Sarah to pop the mold off her face.

When that was done, plaster of Paris was poured into
the alginate mold to make a "positive" of Sarah's face.
When the plaster was hard, Jennifer removed the mold,
set it on a wig stand, and began forming Sarah's Japanese features out of clay.

Sarah did not need a full-face mask, but what she did
need took a steady hand and an artist's eye. Her nose—
small though it was—was too pointed and its bridge too
prominent to be believably Asian. Jen sculpted the clay
to add roundness to the lower planes of Sarah's nose
and build up the sides of the upper bridge so that the
eyelids would flow effortlessly into them. The eyelids
themselves had to both completely cover Sarah's own
and reproduce the epicanthic fold that characterized the
Asian eye while allowing Sarah's eyeball to move
unimpeded.

Once the clay was sculpted, the entire mold—plaster
and clay—was greased, and three separate molds—one
of the nose and one of each eye—were cast from dental
stone, creating positive molds of Sarah's features as they
would look with the prostheses in place. After that, Jennifer removed the clay from the positive, foamed the
latex, and created the latex nose and eyelids using the
positive and negative casts.

As she put the finishing touches on the latex piece,
Jen worried that it wouldn't be good enough. What if it
didn't look real enough and Sarah didn't get nabbed?
Worse, what if someone took her and realized their mistake later? After Travis's call this morning, she wasn't
so confident that the team had come up with the right
plan to flush these guys out.

Sarah stepped out of the bathroom, her new hair swirl-
ing around her shoulders in a wave. The thick black hair
was called China Silk and Jen had spent three hours the
night before gluing it onto Sarah's short straight hair.

"How does this look?"

Jen narrowed her eyes. Sarah had plucked the outside
edges of her eyebrows to eliminate their downward

curve, imitating the short, straight brows of young Japanese girls. Already, the difference was striking.

"Great. There's some ice in the refrigerator, if you want. It'll help take down the swelling."

"I'm okay." Sarah turned from side to side and shook her head. "I still can't believe this hair. It feels like it's my own."

Jennifer nodded. "The adhesives they have now are incredible. When I was working in Vegas, you had to weave in these chunks of hair and they never looked natural up close. With these, you can wash your hair, brush it, even tug on it and they won't come off." She smiled. "Who knows? You might even decide to grow your own hair out."

"Fat chance."

Sarah set her suitcase on the bed and took out a small glass vial.

"Whatcha got there?" Jen asked.

She shrugged and held up a slim white box. "Naloxone, twenty cc's. A hypo."

"The antidote?"

"Yeah. Sub-Q, it should clear an oral dose of morphine out of my system in about an hour."

"What if they don't give you an oral dose?"

Sarah made a fist and pretended to shove the needle into the crook of her arm. "Then I'll just have to find a vein and push the plunger."

Jen nodded. She knew Sarah was talking tough for her sake. Since Travis's call, they'd both been uneasy. Jen wondered what must be going through Sarah's mind.

"Where you gonna stash it?"

Sarah grinned wickedly. "In here." She pulled out a plastic tube, about the size and shape of a small dildo.

Jen's eyes widened. "You're not!"

"Of course I am. Jen, think! Where else am I gonna stick it? If I have it on me they might take it away. This way it'll be with me when I need it and as easy to get to as a tampon. I probably won't stick it in until we get there, though."

Jen grinned. "Why not? It's a long flight. Could be

fun." She nodded toward the latex pieces on her workbench. "You ready for these?"

"As ready as I'll ever be."

Sarah sat down and stared balefully at the paraphernalia Jennifer had laid out on the table: face makeup, lip-
stick, eyebrow pencil, and various tools of the female
trade that she'd spent the better part of her adult life
avoiding.

Jen followed her gaze and smiled, then put a smock
over Sarah's shoulders and opened her FX kit.

"Before I get started, you'll have to put these in." She
handed Sarah two packages containing her brown contact lenses. Sarah opened them up and popped the lenses
into her eyes.

"How do they feel?"

"Okay. How long can I keep these in?"

"They're gas permeable. A week wouldn't kill you.
But we'll have you take them out at night just to give
your eyes a rest."

Sarah picked up a mirror and studied the effect.
"Weird."

Jen reached back into her bag of tricks and took out
a white squeeze bottle.

"This is the surgical adhesive I'll be using to apply the
latex pieces. It's great stuff and it holds like crazy, but
it's going to make removing them uncomfortable. Your
face is going to be a little tender when I take them
off tonight."

"Yeah, well," Sarah snickered, "it won't be the only
place that's tender tonight." She settled back and closed
her eyes. "Go on. Do your worst."

Carefully, Jen set the prostheses over Sarah's eyes and
nose and checked the results. The skin color matched
Sarah's perfectly, and the under eye pieces covered up
most of Sarah's freckles. Jen smiled and nodded. Maybe
this was going to work after all.

An hour later, the latex pieces were on and trimmed
to fit. Jen took out some rubber mask greasepaint,
sponged it onto the latex, then applied makeup to Sarah's face and finished the whole thing with powder. The
effect was stunning.

"Is it over?" Sarah asked.

"Not yet." Jen combed Sarah's hair forward and picked up her scissors.

"What are you doing?"

"Giving you some bangs. It's younger looking and it covers your forehead so you don't notice any difference in skin color." She trimmed Sarah's hair so that the new bangs softly framed her face. "There. Perfect."

Jen handed the mirror to Sarah, who studied herself in awe.

"Shit, Jen, it's great." She looked up. "Maybe I'm not dead after all."

Jen nodded and took the mirror from Sarah's hand.

"You want to talk about it?"

Sarah shrugged. "It's stupid."

"No, it's not. You're scared, okay? I'd be scared, too. We didn't sign up for TALON Force because we wanted to be damsels in distress. We're the strong ones—the ass kickers, not the kickees. You're really brave to let yourself be kidnapped by these guys, especially since . . ."

"Since they might kill me before you guys can find them?"

Jen put her hand on Sarah's. "That won't happen, Sar. I promise. The second they take you, I'll be on their tails like a bloodhound. No way are they going to get away with you. No. Way."

Sarah didn't look convinced.

"Is it the language? Your accent sounded pretty good when I heard you practicing last night."

"No. I've got that part nailed."

"Then what is it? Spit it out, girl. I can't help you if I don't know what the problem is."

Sarah looked out the window at the California sunshine. Three floors below was another world. One where nobody knew or cared about Japanese girls being kidnapped and killed. It was a world she never could—or would want to—be part of again. She looked at Jen.

"The drugs—the mix of alcohol and morphine—it's a lethal combination. Even if that little girl had gotten away, even if she hadn't drowned, she would have OD'd before anyone could have saved her."

"What are you saying? That the antidote won't work?"

"Oh, it'll work all right; but only if I get it into my system fast. If I have to wait more than an hour or two, it might be too late."

"But you said so yourself, you'll have the antidote right there. They give you the drugs and you shoot up. No problem."

"But Jen, what if I'm tied up? What if I can't get my hands free? I can't get the hypo out and stick myself if I'm incapacitated."

Jennifer put her hands on her hips. "What did they use to tie that girl up with?"

"She had hemp fibers in the skin around her wrists."

"Hemp's got more give to it than synthetics. Course, it's scratchy as hell, but you're tough. Houdini wrote the book on escaping from hemp ropes."

"What are you talking about?"

Jen went to the closet and took out her bag of magic props.

"Baby, did I ever tell you about my show in Vegas?"

Chapter Eight

The Lear jet landed at the A.B. Won Pat Guam International Airport and taxied to a stop. Travis looked out at the palm trees that lined the runway and squinted up at the cloudless sky. The sun was straight overhead.

High noon.

Jack stood up and pulled his bag from the back. He slipped on a pair of shades and looked out the window.

"Still another eight hours of daylight," he said. "I'll get a room and see what kind of intel I can find on the streets." He popped the door. "See you all later."

Travis nodded. "Meet us at the Hilton at twenty-one hundred hours local time. Room six eight four."

"Gotcha."

Stan stepped forward and the two of them pushed the gangway out onto the tarmac.

"Go find us some bad guys," he said.

"Will do." Jack turned and clomped down the stairs.

Stan looked at Sam.

"You need help with your bags?"

Sam pushed his glasses up the bridge of his nose. "No. They're not as heavy as they look."

Stan looked at Travis. "I'm heading over to Navstation Marianas to see if I can find a boat. Once I get that squared away, I'll hit the streets with Jack."

"Sounds good. Don't forget—"

"Twenty-one hundred local, room six eight four, the Hilton. Got it." He turned and headed down the gangway.

Travis looked at the other two. "Guess that just leaves the three of us. Sam, I'll get the car and bring it around. Meet me outside in front of the Northwest Air counter."

"Got it."

"Hunter, what's your plan?"

Hunter opened the closet behind the pilot's seat. "I'm going to hang around here for a while, put some feelers out. They've got two more airstrips on the island. I figure I'll give them a look-see, too."

"Good idea. If these guys are flying the girls out, I doubt they're using the airlines."

Travis turned and grabbed the two suitcases that didn't contain Sam's gear. "You two finish up here. Sam, I'll see you outside."

Sam was feeling chatty on the drive to the hotel. Travis could tell he was excited about this mission. Once Sarah was snatched, Sam's communications network would be crucial to their success. He'd been working on the problem of tracking her all day yesterday, he said, and had finally come up with a solution about the same time Travis had dragged in from his evening with Maggie.

Travis smiled, thinking about the trip down to Maalaea Bay in Maggie's truck. They'd parked near the water and walked along the beach at low tide. It had been Maggie's idea to go skinny-dipping. Travis was usually pretty modest about public nudity; but she'd assured him that the area was deserted and the waters warm, and she was right on both counts. Easing into the water had been like slipping into a bath.

They walked out to where the water was waist deep before they even touched each other. Travis said nothing as he followed her deeper into the surf. The stars looked like diamonds on Maggie's wet skin as she strode through the water, her flanks shimmying. Fifty yards out, Maggie turned and threw her hair back, draping her arms around his neck. He cupped her breasts in his hands and kissed them, one after the other, then her mouth. She reached down into the water and took him firmly in her hand. He closed his eyes and let out an involuntary moan. Then she lifted her leg and wrapped it around his back and he took her ass in his hands. In an instant, he was inside her—

"Boss, have you heard a word I said?"

Travis roused himself from his daydream. Sam was giving him a puzzled look.

"What's wrong?"

"Nothing. Just thinking." No sense telling the kid what he'd missed. Travis had a feeling Sam wouldn't understand.

"Like I was saying, to use the implant as a homing device, it needs to be reprogrammed."

"That's not so hard, is it? I've had mine reprogrammed before."

"I know; but I need to override the radio. The chip needs to remain in transmit mode without being touched."

"So what did you decide to do?"

"I came up with a way to change the implant so that it transmits a constant, low frequency signal that we can use to track Sarah anywhere she goes. I even made a device that can boost her signal in case she gets too far away. I've got it in my bags." He threw a thumb in the direction of the trunk. "That's what I was doing last night while you animals were out deflowering the locals."

Travis shook his head. "Sam, what would we do without you?"

"Land yourself in deep doo-doo, that's what."

The Guam Hilton was on the right. Travis signaled and turned into the parking garage.

"You talk to the others last night?"

"Yeah. I told them I didn't want to lose Sarah because they didn't take the mission seriously."

"What did they say?"

Travis took a ticket at the kiosk and started searching for a spot.

"They understood."

Sam shook his head. "I don't know. I don't think their hearts are in it."

"You're wrong, Sam. If I know this team, those guys are out there right now, busting their humps."

Chapter Nine

Hunter put his jacket on and closed up the jet. It was a nice little bird, good for what it was designed for—speed and comfort—but the Lear was as soulless as a vampire. As far as Hunter was concerned, the days of the great planes were over—had been for years. He hated to admit it but Stan was right. Flying a plane these days was like driving a bus.

He walked across the tarmac wondering what he should do first. Sam had already tapped into the airport's databases, checking the passenger lists for all commercial flights off the island in the last six months, and come up with nothing. The best thing to do now would be to ask around and see if anyone had seen anything suspicious on one of the private flights. Ground crews had notoriously loose lips. He wanted to find out how easy it would be to take someone off the island unannounced.

There was a private hangar a hundred yards north of where Hunter had left the Lear—a domed, three-story structure made of corrugated metal, with a huge opening on one end where planes could enter for repairs. A small office—more of a lean-to with windows—had been tacked onto its side. But Hunter wasn't there on official business. He bypassed the office and walked right into the shop.

The place smelled like grease and avgas, and it was cool inside—at least 10 degrees cooler than out on the runway. Hunter figured that'd change as the day wore on. By late afternoon, this place would feel like an oven.

The sound of clanging metal reverberated through the

cavernous hangar. Most of the planes inside were beat-up old Cessna amphibs—puddle hoppers being readied for their next commute between the islands. The old sea planes had character, Hunter thought, but they were draft horses. Hunter's tastes ran more toward thorough-breds.

Off to his right, a man was riveting a flap back onto the wing of a DeHavilland Beaver. As the man carefully positioned his rivet gun, Hunter considered his next move.

Technically, private pilots were supposed to declare all passengers aboard in the same way that commercial flights did; but in reality, the authorities didn't always check to see if the manifest matched up with the actual number of passengers. Hunter figured he'd see if he could chat up some of the ground crews, find out if there was anyone who habitually fudged on their declarations.

In his pocket, Hunter carried a driver's license and ID for Redmond Flagg, inspector for the Federal Aviation Administration. The name, "Red" Flagg, was one of Sam's jokes—an alias he'd slipped into the FAA's data-base. If anyone questioned the credentials of Mr. Flagg, they'd find the administration did, indeed, have him on their personnel rosters, even if no one could recall hav-ing ever met him. Of course, Hunter preferred going in on friendly terms; but it was nice to know he could be a hard-ass if he needed to be.

Now all he had to do was find someone who would talk to him.

A small Filipino man in coveralls walked up and gave Hunter a nod before he began rooting through a box of tools. He made no attempt to ask Hunter what his busi-ness there was. Apparently, security here was pretty lax.

Hunter smiled and stepped forward. "Hi. I've got a little problem I was hoping you could help me with."

"Sure," the man said, pulling a rag from his back pocket and wiping his hand. "If I can."

Hunter pointed toward the Lear jet. "I just got in. That's my bird out there."

The little man glanced back over Hunter's shoulder

and nodded his approval. "Nice plane. What's the problem?"

"Well," Hunter said, lowering his voice and looking around. "I've got a little discrepancy in the manifest."

The man's eyes widened.

"Don't get excited. It's not drugs. Just an extra passenger who'd rather nobody knew he was here. Know anyone who could help me out?"

The man shook his head. "Not here, man. FAA will pull your license if you don't declare him."

Hunter frowned and feigned consternation. "Damn. That really puts me in a bind." He reached for his wallet. "I don't suppose you'd know anybody at one of the smaller strips who could give me a hand." He pulled out a fifty and held it discreetly for the man to see.

The mechanic glanced around and took the fifty. "Yeah, I might know somebody."

"Does he have a name?"

"Carlos. He owns a little strip over on the east side of the island—MacArthur Airpark. I've heard he knows how to help a guy in a jam."

"Is the strip long enough for me to land my bird?"

"He's had a few small jets in there before. I think you could manage it."

Hunter nodded. "Carlos. MacArthur. Thanks."

"Don't mention it. If you need to file a new flight plan, Brad can do that for you in the office. It'll save you some time."

"I'll do that. Thanks."

He walked out of the huge hangar door and around the corner to the office. Inside, an older man with a deep tan and a full head of white hair was sitting behind a cheap metal desk, talking on the telephone. He wore a loud, Hawaiian print shirt and had a booming voice, and he waved Hunter toward an ancient secretary's chair as he continued his conversation. Hunter took a seat and looked around.

This was a nice place—clean and neat, if a little worn. Hunter often wondered what he'd do with himself once his military days were over. Owning a little business like this might be fun. He could make the rounds of the air shows during the summer and rent himself out as a test pilot when things got dull. During the fall and winter, he could make ends meet giving flying lessons to rich men's wives. Sounded pretty good.

The older man hung up the phone and swiveled in his chair. "Sorry to keep you waiting." He stuck out his hand. "Brad LeRoy."

Hunter took his outstretched hand. "Redmond Flagg."

"Nice to meet you, Red. You take a lot of grief for that handle?"

"All the time."

"What can I do for you?"

"I just flew in from Hawaii and I need to make a hop over to MacArthur. Your mechanic told me I could file my flight plan with you."

"Absolutely," Brad said, turning to his computer. "We've got the tower on-line here. Let me see when I can get you a slot." He entered his name and password and turned back toward Hunter. "What kind of crate you flying?"

"A Lear."

"Nice bird."

"It's okay. I'm on taxi duty this week."

Brad nodded sympathetically. "Pretty damned cushy." He checked the screen. "When do you want to leave?"

"As soon as you can put me in the air."

Brad typed in a few words and waited for a response. "What else do you fly?"

"Anything with wings—Pipers, Fokkers, jets. Been flying since I was ten."

The man turned. "Fokkers? No kidding?"

"Nope. Got a summer job at Rhinebeck Aerodrome in upstate New York when I was in high school. Flew a replica of the Red Baron's triplane. In my spare time, I play around in a little ultralight I had built to my own specs. I think I've spent more of my life in the air than on the ground."

The man gave him a penetrating look. "How'd you manage all that in such a short life?"

Hunter kept a poker face. "Air Force brat."

Brad raised an eyebrow. "Of course." He looked at the screen again. "They've got an opening in half an hour."

"I'll take it. Thanks."

"No problem." The man scheduled the time and put the computer to sleep. "Have you got a minute, Red? I think I've got something in the back that might interest you."

Hunter hesitated.

"It'll only take a minute."

"Sure. Why not?"

The two men headed out the door and walked back into the hangar, bypassing the mechanic and the man with the welding torch, going deeper into the body of the building. Every nook and cranny was littered with the bodies of broken planes, some of them antique, most of them merely old. It felt like they were moving through a graveyard.

"This is where I keep my toys," Brad said. He pointed toward a pile of rusted metal plane parts. "That'll be a Boeing P-26 once I get it cleaned up and reassembled."

Hunter nodded appreciatively. "The Peashooter."

"That's right. And over there," Brad pointed, "I've got a Republic P-47 Thunderbolt."

Hunter stepped over and examined the partially assembled plane. It wasn't much to look at yet, but it would be. If he used his imagination, Hunter could almost see the fighter bomber diving toward Japanese targets in the Pacific.

"Not hard to see why they called it the flying milk bottle."

Brad chuckled. "She'll never win a beauty contest, that's for sure; but she did a good job for us when we needed her."

"Are all your planes from World War Two?"

Brad nodded. "That was my war. Had to lie about my age to get into it; but it was worth it. Some of the best memories of my life are of flying over the Pacific in a jug like this." He grinned. "But you haven't seen the best one yet."

The two men stepped into another part of the hangar.

One that had been separated from the rest of the shop by ten-foot high baffles. Through an opening in the partition, Hunter caught sight of the plane inside and his heart leaped. Forgetting his host, he hurried forward.

Brad's face split into a wide grin. "You like it? It's a—"

"Grumman JRF Goose," Hunter said reverently. "An amphib flying boat."

The plane was sitting in the middle of an open area, its wheels chocked, looking like the day it rolled off the Grumman assembly line in Bethpage, New York. Its curved fuselage was a perfect blend of air- and watercraft and two pontoons hung from the single, fixed wing. Every inch of the plane had been lovingly restored, right down to the World War II vintage paint job. Hunter walked a slow perimeter around it.

"Rate of climb at sea level was eleven hundred feet per minute—service ceiling's at twenty-one thousand." He stopped at the wing. "Two four fifty horsepower R-nine-eight-five-AN-six engines. It could go six hundred and forty miles on one tank of gas."

Hunter turned and looked at the older man. "Where did you get it?"

Brad LeRoy smiled and scratched the back of his head. "Now that's an interesting story. I bought it at an auction ten years ago. The guy who owned it passed away before he could restore it and his widow had no idea what she had on her hands, so she just let it go to hell. It wasn't until she died that the family decided to get rid of it. It was a rust bucket when I purchased it; I've spent a bundle and the last decade of my life rebuilding it. She's fully restored."

Hunter reached up and ran his hand along the wing.

"You want to take her up?"

He shook his head. "No time now. Wish I could, though."

"You sure? You can do it when you get back from MacArthur."

"No. No, I've got work to do."

The older man nodded. "Well, let me know if you

change your mind. It might not be around here much longer."

"Why not?"

"I'm selling it."

"After all the time and money you've put into it?"

LeRoy shook his head sadly. "I'm not a young man anymore, Red. Next year this time, I'll be retired."

"But you'll still be flying."

"Oh, sure. But not this crate. It's not an easy bird to handle. I found that out after I got her all put back together. No, it takes a special pilot to fly this baby." He smiled ruefully. "Guess I thought maybe you were the one."

Hunter swallowed, feeling oddly guilty. "Well, thanks for thinking of me."

"You bet." The old man looked at his watch. "You'd better get out to your bird. Tower's going to want you on the runway pretty soon. Guess I kept you longer than I said I would."

"No problem." Hunter reached out and shook the old man's hand. "This was worth it."

Chapter Ten

Guam might be a tropical paradise, Jack thought, but every city had its seamy side; and Agana was no exception. Didn't matter if it was Atlanta—where Jack grew up—or New Delhi, or Dar es Salaam; anywhere a dozen people or more lived together somebody always ended up at the bottom of the pile. He looked around at the filthy streets, the garbage strewn alleyways, and the littered sidewalks. It felt like home.

Jack's first stop after leaving the airport had been a fleabag hotel on Fifth Street, where he'd rented a room and dropped off his stuff. He'd spent a few minutes talking with the manager, a fat old Tahitian lady with skin so tight he thought her cheeks would split open every time she smiled, then headed out onto the streets to see what scuttlebutt he might be able to find on the ten little Japanese girls.

Jack felt like a fish out of water walking around, wondering what to do. He knew Travis wanted them to take this assignment seriously, but the whole thing sucked. He hadn't joined TALON Force to be some two-bit James Bond. Hell, he couldn't even use his high-tech snoopers out here; if he got caught, it'd be TALON's ass. The whole mission was starting to feel like a goatfuck.

He was dressed for the balmy day in a tight T-shirt, cutoff Levis, and Air Jordans; he strutted while he walked, hoping that with his muscular physique and no-

shit-taking attitude someone would take him for an ex-
con. It worked. Decent-looking folks who saw him coming crossed the street, but the rest—the ones he needed
to talk to—watched him with a glint of self-interest in
their eyes. What did this man want, and how much
would he pay for it?

It didn't take much to fall back into the pose, of
course. Jack had spent his childhood as a junior thug,
training for the big time. Only the intervention of a sympathetic judge had saved him from a life of crime. Abra-
ham Wilkins was the first male authority figure the
young Jacques DuBois had ever met, and the first black
man he'd ever seen in a courtroom who wasn't on trial.
The tough ex-Marine saw something in Jack that Jack
had never seen in himself: potential. Wilkins's offer the
day Jack came into his courtroom was simple: reform
school or the Marines. Jack chose the Corps and had
never regretted it a day since. Especially now, when he
could see what his life would have ended up like the
other way.

Yes sir. But sometimes a brother needed to get back
to his roots.

He turned south at the next corner and continued his
recon of the area. The streets were laid out in a grid
that followed the four points of the compass, and even
in this part of town they were in good shape. Closer to
the waterfront, there'd been some newer buildings and
a few pricey restaurants; but the farther he got from the
water, the worse shape the buildings were in. By the
time he was ten blocks from the bay, the nice apartments
and upscale shops had given way to porno houses and
derelict tenements. For the last three hours, he'd been
stopping at bars and asking about the girls. This was the
last one.

The sign on the door said: YOU MUST BE OVER 18 TO
ENTER. Jack could hear music inside, but the windows
had been painted out and the porthole in the wooden
door wasn't big enough to see into. He pushed the door
open and stepped inside.

The place reeked of stale smoke with an unmistakable
mixture of puke and Lysol. Someone had taken a piss

on the threshold and the smell followed Jack in through the door.

The bar was a wooden plank about ten feet long mounted on the righthand wall, with a couple of mismatched stools huddled underneath. Two tables in the room shared five chairs between them. Two men sat at the far end of the bar, hunkered over their drinks. Neither one seemed in any mood to talk. Behind the bar stood an old man—probably the owner—a white guy with sunken cheeks, stringy black hair that looked like he dyed it with shoe polish, and a dingy plastic lei around his neck. The entire establishment probably measured no more than twenty by twenty.

Jack walked up to the bar and ordered a Black and White. He glanced around.

"Kinda quiet 'round here."

"This is a quiet town," the man said, handing him his glass.

"I'm starting to believe that." Jack took a gulp of the heavily watered Scotch. "I'm looking for some girls."

"No girls in here," the man said, shaking his head. "Girls mean trouble. We don't want no cops coming around. You want girls, you go to Madame Cho's."

"No," Jack said, shaking his head. "I'm not looking for that kind of girl. I'm talking about young girls. Japanese. You heard of any around here?"

The old man shook his head. "Not any kind of girls around here. All we got here is music and booze."

Great. Another dead end.

Jack put down his drink and stood up. "Thanks anyway."

Back out on the sidewalk again, Jack headed down the street the way he'd come, sweeping his eyes from side to side, watching for any of the same faces he'd seen before. The wrong side of the tracks was only so big on this island. What did he have to do, send up a flare?

He walked to the end of the block and turned south toward downtown. If they'd just let him use his eye-in-the-sky, he could have this place reconned in no time and can this gumshoe bullshit.

"Yo, brother. What's happenin'?"

Jack stopped and smiled—bingo!—then turned slowly around.

It was a skinny, redheaded, white kid with dreadlocks and a mouthful of ganja-stained teeth. Jack hid his revulsion behind a scowl.

"What's the word, my man? How's it hangin'?" The kid was shucking and jiving, his locks swaying around his shoulders. His eyes were wide; Jack figured he must be hopped up on something.

"It's cool," Jack said. What was with this kid and his Superfly soundtrack?

"I hear you're lookin' for some girls, bro."

Jack nodded. "You heard right. You know where I can find some?"

"Maybe so. Maybe so. What's it worth to you?"

Jack hesitated. He hadn't planned on spending a lot of money on bribes. In his pockets, he had maybe a hundred bucks and change.

"Fifty enough?"

"Don't know. Sometimes my memory's not what it used to be. Fact is, though, if I don't know where your little Japanese girls are, nobody else in this town does."

Jack nodded. Someone in one of the bars must have tipped this kid off.

"All right, how 'bout I give you fifty now and another fifty when I see the girls."

"Sounds fair. Sounds very fair," the kid said, swaying to some unknown rhythm. "Yes sir, this be your lucky day for sure."

Jack was getting tired of this guy. "Okay, here's your fifty. Let's go."

The young man snatched the bill away and tucked it deep into his pants.

"No, no. Can't go. Not now. Not with everybody lookin'." He glanced around suspiciously. "You meet me here later. Two hours. I'll take you to your girls."

Jack grabbed the kid's shirt and pulled him up short. In two hours, and with fifty bucks in his pocket, this guy could get high enough to forget he'd ever even met Jack.

"You not shittin' me are you?"

The kid was trembling. "No way, man. You're my bro. I'll be here. Take you to the girls. Get my other fifty."

"Okay," Jack said, releasing him. "I'll see you then."

The young man practically tripped over his own feet trying to get away. As Jack watched him go, he had a feeling he'd never see the kid again.

Damn!

He checked his watch. It was three-twenty. Two hours would give him just enough time to head over to Chamorro Village and check out the place where the first girl was abducted. Maybe while he was there he could get something to eat. He didn't want to have to look at that kid's teeth again on an empty stomach.

Chapter Eleven

Travis stood listening at the wall, waiting for the maid to leave the connecting room. In another few hours, when Jennifer and Sarah arrived, it would be theirs; but Sam had commandeered every square inch of their room, and right now he needed a place to work.

There was equipment scattered everywhere around the hotel room: a computer on the table, a satellite dish on the balcony, speakers, an amplifier, and an extra hard drive on the dresser, DVDs, a video card, and a mag reader on the beds. Cables were draped over everything. Sam was oblivious to the mess, but Travis couldn't operate like that. Besides, every power strip in the room was already being used and he had to charge up the battle ensembles. He needed to get into the other room to get some power.

He heard the click of the door on the other side—the maid was leaving—and looked at Sam.

"Sammy, can you make that key for me now?"

Sam was ensconced behind his computer. "Just a second. I'm patching into the hotel's computer now."

A few keystrokes later, he was nodding at the screen. "Okay, we're in. Give me your card."

Travis handed him his key card—the one that opened this room—and Sam inserted it into his mag read/write machine. With the room codes in the central computer, Sam could write any one of them onto Travis's card— in this case, giving him access to the room next door.

The device hummed for an instant and Sam removed the card.

"Here," he said. "Give it a try."

Travis stepped out into the hallway and inserted the key card into the reader on the door. The status light turned from red to green.

"Bingo."

He turned the handle and walked inside. The women's room was a mirror image of the one he and Sam were sharing: a bathroom, two double beds, a table, dresser, TV, and a sitting area off to the side with a couch, a refrigerator, and another television.

Travis shook his head. It never ceased to amaze him that people would travel thousands of miles to a tropical paradise just to sit in front of a TV.

He walked to the connecting door and opened it. Sam was under the table, messing with some cables on the ground. Travis stepped through the room and grabbed their Low Observable Camouflage Suites—suits, gloves, and boots—from his footlocker. If Sarah was kidnapped tomorrow, the LOCSs would have to be charged up and ready to go. He took out two charging couplers and walked back into the women's room, plugging one into the electrical outlet by the bed. There were only two plugs in the whole room—this one and the one in the bathroom—and it took an hour to charge each suite. The Hyper-Capacitor belts kept their charges and could be used for up to thirty minutes of auxiliary power; but if the team needed them for longer than that, each item of the suites themselves would have to be charged separately.

When the first two suites were ready, Travis hung them in the closet in his room and checked to see if Sam needed any help. A few times in the last hour, he'd heard an earsplitting stream of profanity coming from their room and he needed to reassure himself that Sam had the communications network under control.

"How's it going in here?"

Sam poked his head out from under the table. "In what sense?"

Travis shrugged. "You're the computer geek. Is this stuff working yet?"

Sam frowned thoughtfully. "Not yet. Not enough juju. Maybe if you could sacrifice a live chicken, things would go faster."

"That's supposed to be funny, right?"

"It goes over big at MacWorld."

Travis shook his head and went back to charging the LOCSs.

The suites were really the slickest part of the TALON Force Battle Ensemble. Using micro-sensors woven into their fabric, the camo suits could determine the visual qualities of their surroundings and blend in automatically. This chameleonlike quality made the LOCSs a little tricky to keep track of, though. A fully charged suite, once activated, could easily be lost if it was removed, leaving the owner with no recourse other than to grope around blindly trying to reacquire it or wait until it lost its charge and became visible again. The whole situation just reinforced Travis's suspicion that technology was only as good as the stupidest man using it.

While the second set of suites charged up, Travis took his weapons out, broke them down, and laid them out on the beds. He went over each one, inspecting every component and cleaning it carefully. There were still too many variables he had no control over on this mission. Every time he could take care of one he did have control over, he felt better.

"Travis, can you give me a hand in here?"

"Sure. Just a second." He put the last of the pieces together and gathered up his weapons. When he did come face-to-face with the unfriendlies, at least he knew he could count on his firepower.

He walked into the room and put them away.

"What can I help you with?"

Sam was lying on his back under the table amid a tangle of wires and coaxial cables. His mouth was pressed together in a thin, angry line as he sorted through them.

"I need to label these spaghetti strands," he huffed, "before I chuck the whole thing out the window."

"Okay. What can I do?"

"Stand over here by the computer and watch the con-nectors on the back. When one of the cables moves, tell me where it's plugged in so I can put a label on it. Okay?"

"Can do." Travis leaned over and took a gander at the back of the computer. A dozen wires were running into and out of it and into the various boxes and doo-dads scattered all over the room. No wonder Sam was hot. Following where this stuff went was like running a maze with your eyes.

One of the wires moved.

"Okay," Travis said. "That one's connected to the first hole on the left."

"Which left? My left or your left?"

"Uh, my left when I'm looking directly at the back of the computer."

"Are you looking over the top?"

"No."

"Okay then; that's the modem port."

"Isn't that what I said?"

Travis heard the maid outside, pushing her cart down the hallway.

"How about this one?" Sam asked.

Another cable moved. Travis was about to say which one when he heard the unmistakable click of the con-necting room door.

"Oh shit!"

"What's the matter?"

"The maid! She's going into the girls' room."

Travis sprinted through the door and grabbed the suite out of the bathroom, then snatched the other one off the bed. The maid was backing into the room, pulling her linen cart behind her; she hadn't seen or heard him yet. He threw the suites back into his room and closed the door behind him.

"Did you get the suites?"

"Yeah. I think so."

Travis picked up the pieces and set them carefully on the bed. In his haste, he'd accidentally activated one of the suits, making it difficult to separate out.

"Okay. Two suits, two gloves, one . . . Shit! I left one of the boots in there."

"Well, you can't get it now."

"The hell I can't."

Travis pulled out his battle helmet, turned on the thermal sensor, and stared at the wall. The signal was faint, but it appeared the maid had gone into the bathroom. He got down on all fours and opened the door.

The boot was on the floor between the bed and Travis. The thing had been activated, but a faint glimmer in the viewing screen confirmed its position. Travis opened the door another inch hoping to grab the boot, but before he could get close enough, the maid stepped out of the bathroom. He scrambled back into the room and shut the door a second time.

"Did you get it?"

"No."

Sam peered out from under the table. "If she finds it, we're in deep shit."

"Yeah," Travis said, "I know." He sat down and closed his eyes.

Please God, don't let me fuck up this mission.

A minute later, the women's room was empty again. Travis opened the door and retrieved the boot—the maid must not have seen it—then stored it in the closet with the others before returning to the table to help Sam.

When all the cables were labeled and accounted for, Sam gave Travis a tour.

"The heart of the system is this customized Power-Book," he said, patting the laptop computer proudly. "It's got a gigabyte of RAM plus a built-in DVD-ROM drive with a video processor card and a satellite connection with a range of eight hundred miles."

"Impressive," Travis said, not 100 percent sure what any of it meant.

"From here, I can access the output data from each of your helmets while you're in the field and send impulses between each member to help you coordinate your offensive. I can see what you see and hear what you hear. Wherever you go, I'll be right with you."

"What about Sarah's implant?"

"The signal's pretty weak; but I've got a special filtering program that will help me pick out her signal as long as she doesn't get too far away."

"Don't worry. As soon as she gets nabbed, we'll be on her tail."

"Good. Even with her signal boosted, her implant can't transmit much farther than a quarter mile or so."

"That should be plenty of room."

"Then we're set. All we have to do is wait until they take her."

"Which reminds me." Travis checked his watch. "The girls should have checked in by now."

Sam nodded. "Let me check the computer." He sat down and brought up the hotel's main menu.

"Let's see . . . current guest list . . ." He punched a few keys and pointed at the screen. "They're here. And . . . someone just pressed the sixth floor button in elevator number two; my guess is that's them."

A minute later, Travis heard the lock in the adjoining room click. He and Sam waited for the bellboy to bring in the women's baggage, then let themselves in through the connecting door.

As she stepped into the room, Travis stopped dead in his tracks.

Jen was standing in the middle of the room, dressed like a schoolmarm in a shapeless lavender dress and thick glasses. Her lush mane of blonde hair had been dyed brown and pulled back into a bun and the padding around her midsection gave the illusion of fifty extra pounds. Next to her stood a tiny Japanese princess in a school uniform.

Sam stepped forward.

"Konichi-wa," he said, bowing respectfully.

"Konichi-wa," the girl said in a soft voice.

"Hajimemashite." Nice to meet you.

She lowered her eyes. *"Arigato."* Thank you. *"Dochirahe?"* How are you?

"Junchou." Okay. Sam nodded. "Nice accent. Tokyo by way of New England prep."

The girl's face twisted into a smirk. *"Kutabare!"*

Sam's mouth fell open. "Who taught you that?"

Sarah bowed toward Jen. "Honorable chaperon."

Travis had watched the entire exchange, awestruck. Now, hearing Sarah's own voice, the spell was broken. He looked at Sam.

"What did she say?"

"She told me to go fuck myself!"

Travis laughed. "My God, Sarah. It really is you."

"Of course it is. Don't you recognize me?"

He shook his head, circling her slowly. The face, the hair, even the body seemed so tiny and delicate. Who could guess that a full-fledged Army ranger was hidden under all that makeup?

"I don't think your own mother would recognize you."

"Good. Let's hope the kidnappers agree." She walked into the bathroom and closed the door.

Travis looked at Jen. "Rough flight?"

"Not bad. We had to be ready for anything before we got here. She needs a second to unpack the antidote."

Travis raised his eyebrows questioningly and Jen shook her head.

"You don't need to know." She reached up and undid the bun, fluffing her hair.

"How's she doing?"

"She's okay. Nervous; but then, we all are. I showed her how to get loose from a rope tie—that was worrying her. She's been better since then."

Jennifer held her arms out. "Well? You didn't say anything about my getup. What do you think? I was going for a sort of Marian the Librarian look."

Travis shook his head. "I don't think I ever knew any librarians that looked like you."

"Yeah. There wasn't enough time to do much with myself." She shrugged. "Oh well. Kidnapping isn't rocket science. With any luck, these guys will never wonder what a Japanese schoolgirl is doing with an Anglo governess."

The bathroom door opened and Sarah walked out.

"Any food around here? I'm starved."

"There's a good restaurant downstairs, or you can call

room service," Travis said. "Sam's been living out of the vending machines."

Sarah flopped down on the bed and picked up the phone. "I'll take room service. I don't feel like going out again."

While she was on the phone, the others walked into Sam and Travis's room. Jennifer's eyes popped at the sight of Sam's command and control setup.

"My God, Sam! What's all this?"

Sam rocked back on his heels. "You know what they say: a man can never be too rich or too well-equipped."

"Well, that much is true." She looked at Travis. "Where are the other guys?"

"Hunter's checking out the airports; Jack's doing recon; and Stan called right after we checked in and said he was going to meet with some old SEAL buddies to see if we could borrow their boat."

"They've got a team on the island?"

"Apparently so. Team Five just got back from joint maneuvers in the Philippines. They won't be heading home for a few days yet."

Jennifer frowned. "Which means they'll be in a party mode."

"Don't worry," Travis said. "Stan knows we've got a meeting here at twenty-one hundred. He'll keep himself under control."

Chapter Twelve

The contest was simple—to see which man could do the most push-ups with a girl sitting on his back. If Stan won, he got to use the SEALs' boat, a Mark V Special Operations Patrol Boat. If the other guy won, he got Stan's wallet—along with the two thousand dollars Travis had given him to secure a civilian transport. There was no time limit, but the push-ups had to be done one after another—no stopping to catch your breath. The girls had been weighed and the lighter one was holding a bottle of champagne, to be poured over the winner's head when the contest was over.

Stan's rider was a tiny Guamanian girl with cocoa brown skin and hazel eyes who sat cross-legged on his spine. They'd been groping each other for over an hour; but Stan didn't want to leave the party just for some pussy. It wasn't just that there was money riding on this, either. SEAL Team Five's current leader, Gus Jarvis, was an old rival of Stan's and the contest had gotten started when Gus claimed that Stan's new assignment had left him soft. He'd dared Stan to go head-to-head with him for the use of the Mark V. And Stan Powczuk never backed down from a dare.

Now, stretched out face down, toes and fingers on the floor, waiting for the signal, Stan tried not to think about how much trouble he was going to be in when Travis found out.

If Travis found out.

The bar's owner—who'd agreed to referee the contest when it was clear he couldn't stop it—stepped up in front of the competitors and checked their payloads, then made sure all bets were in place. He raised his arm.

"On your marks, get set, go!"

Stan began pumping his arms up and down. The girl on his back felt like nothing. All around him, the SEAL team members were calling out cadence:

"A-one, a-two, a-three . . ."

He could have gone faster, but it was easier to stick to a rhythm. The going would get hard soon enough. No sense inviting trouble.

The girl on his back shifted and Stan yelled.

"Get back up on my shoulders! You're rocking the boat!"

She moved again and perched just between his shoulder blades.

"Ah," he sighed. "That feels nice."

Fifty push-ups went by like a breeze. Stan didn't even break a sweat till he was almost to a hundred. Out of the corner of his eye, he saw Gus still pumping, his hands and face turning red. Stan grinned and redoubled his effort.

A hundred and sixty. A hundred and seventy. Now he was starting to feel the girl on his back. Two hundred. What was she doing back there, eating a platter of ribs?

Gus hadn't slowed down, but Stan could see the sweat dripping off his face and hitting the barroom floor. Sweat was getting in his own eyes, too. Stan growled and shook his head like a dog, sending warm salty droplets in all directions.

The cadence had slowed by the time they reached three hundred. Every push-up took three times as long going up as coming down and the muscles in Stan's arms were beginning to shake. He didn't know how many more push-ups he'd be able to do. Team Five was down on all fours, slamming their fists on the ground, egging Gus on. No one had bet on Stan. No one really expected to part with the boat.

Shit for brains.

Three hundred and twenty-five. Every pump now was

agony. Stan strained, his arms shaking so hard the girl on his back had to hold on to his shirt to keep from falling. Three hundred and twenty-six. He gasped for breath, locking his elbows at the top for a millisecond to give his shoulders some relief. Gus was hurting, too. Stan heard him groan as he finished another one. It wasn't over yet.

Two more. Then another. Stan felt like he was going to die. He gritted his teeth and pushed up again. His arms were on fire. How many was that? Was he ahead or was Gus? Who was keeping count?

He lowered himself again and tried to push. His whole body quivered as he willed his arms to straighten.

"Come on!" he yelled.

Beside him, Gus was doing the same.

"Who's ahead?!" Stan screamed.

"Nobody!" the bartender yelled.

This was it, then. They were both exhausted, both on the verge of collapse. Whoever made it to the top this time would win. Stan's arms were still shaking, but he was inching skyward. On his right, Gus was still moving, too. What if they both made it to the top? What then? Stan didn't think he had another one in him.

He made it. Stan locked his elbows, then turned and looked at Gus. The SEAL's face was purple and the veins bulged on his forearms as he strained. He got half-way there, then another inch . . .

And collapsed. Face down, nose in the floorboards, out for the count. Stan unlocked his elbows, tucked his right arm under, and fell onto his shoulder. The Guamanian girl shrieked and jumped off as he rolled onto his back and stared at the ceiling. The crowd was cheering—even Gus's SEALs. Stan put his hands on his forehead and took a deep breath, then rolled onto his side and puked.

"Hey," one of the SEALs laughed. "Maybe his name should be Upchuck, not Powczuk!"

But Stan didn't care. He saw stars. He felt dizzy. There was sweat in his eyes and vomit on his chin.

He'd never been so happy in his life.

Then Stan heard a pop and saw a stream of foam fly.

He opened his mouth and caught some champagne as it splashed over his face and neck. He'd done it: beaten Gus in front of his own men *and* secured a Mark V for the mission. Tomorrow, if anybody took Sarah, TALON Force could follow them in the best damned boat afloat.

Stan checked his watch: twenty forty-two. *Shit!* He'd have to haul ass if he was going to get to the hotel on time. He sat up. Gus was sitting up too, his arms wrapped around his midsection.

Stan stood on wobbly legs and bent down, putting his face in Gus's.

"Oh, Da-a-ad. Can I have the keys to the car now?"

Gus sneered; but a bet was a bet. He took out a card with the key code for the Mark V on it and handed it to Stan.

"Gee thanks, Pops. I'll try to have it back by midnight."

Stan shoved the card into his wallet and headed out the door.

Chapter Thirteen

At twenty-one-oh-three hours, the team assembled in the women's room. Jack sat on the couch next to Jennifer, Sarah sat on her bed; Hunter Blake had commandeered a chair and Stan was on the floor, reeking of puke and alcohol. Sam stayed on his feet, leaning against the wall by the connecting door.

Travis looked around and cleared his throat.

"Tomorrow's the big day," he said. "Sarah and Jen are going to hit the streets at oh-nine-hundred hours and start trawling for kidnappers. In a minute, you can give me your status reports; but first, let me tell you about some things that Sam's been working on.

"Sarah's implant has been reprogrammed to act like a homing device. As of now, she can't hear from or talk to any of you out in the field, so if you need to get a message to her, send it to Jen. Once Sarah's been taken, Sam will use his console to tell us where she is.

"Next, since you can't use your helmets out on the streets, Sam's got transceiver/battery arrays for each of you to put in your pockets." He turned to Sam, who held one of the matchbook-size arrays in the air. "They'll boost your implant's output so the rest of us can pick it up from anywhere on the island. They'll also transmit anything you say back up here to command and control.

"While you're out there, I'll be monitoring your movements from up here. As soon as Sarah gets nabbed, I'll

give each of you the coordinates you'll need to vector
into her position and stick with her. When we find out
where they're keeping the rest of the girls, we'll move
in and shut down the operation." He looked around.
"Any questions?"

There were none.

"All right. Hunter, what did you find out at the
airport?"

Hunter swiveled in his seat. "Getting the girls out on
a private plane from Guam International might be do-
able, but not easy. I took a hop over to a strip on the
east side called MacArthur Air, though, and the place is
pretty lax. There's a possibility the girls could be taken
out there."

"Did you check their records?"

"I did. If they're accurate, there haven't been any
flights out in the last six months that correspond to any
of the abductions. That's not to say they couldn't have
been fudged; but I told them I was FAA, and they didn't
even flinch."

"Jack, what's the word on the streets?"

"Not much," Jack said. "I covered some major ground
and didn't come up with squat."

"How about that kid you mentioned when you came
in?"

"He never showed. I'll keep an eye out when I'm on
the streets again. Might be something there."

Stan glanced at him. "What kid?"

"Some skinny-ass white dude copping a Bob Marley.
Said he knows where the girls are."

"Does he?"

"Don't know. I paid him fifty bucks and he ran off."
He looked at Travis. "I can go back and look for him
tomorrow, if you want."

Travis shook his head. "Don't bother. I think our orig-
inal plan's a good one. Let's give Sarah and Jen a chance
to lure these guys into the open. Then we'll know for
sure we're dogging the right rabbit." He looked at Stan.
"You want to tell us what you've been up to?"

Stan crossed his arms and grinned broadly. "I got us
a boat."

"I gathered that much. What kind?"

"The best fucking boat in the whole goddamned world, that's what: a Mark Five." He extended his arms and stuck out his thumbs and index fingers like a filmmaker framing a shot.

"Picture this: eighty-five feet of sleek gray metal. Goes fifty-five plus in the open ocean and has a Combat Rubber Raiding Craft that launches off the back. A covered cabin, four weapons stations with machine guns and grenade launchers, and an extra-large fuel tank for over-the-horizon ops." He dropped his hands and settled back. "You may now bow down and worship me."

"Sounds like a lot of boat."

"Yeah, Stan," Jen said. "How'd you get them to loan it to you?"

"Hey, us SEALs stick together. Besides, I earned it fair and square."

"Yes," Hunter said dryly. "I'm sure you did."

"All right," Travis said. "Sounds like we're covered." He looked at Sarah. "How are you doing?"

She shook her head. "Don't worry about me. I'm packing the antidote with me and Jen's got ten more doses for the girls in her rucksack."

"Good work. Okay, Sam's got something he wants to tell us, so listen up."

Travis sat down and Sam stepped away from the wall, folding his hands behind his back.

"Ever since General Krauss gave us this assignment, I've been trying to figure out when the next girls would be taken. I'm pretty sure I now know what the correlation is.

"It wasn't easy. For one thing, the abductions have been going on longer than Krauss said."

"Why would he lie to us?" Jen asked.

"I don't think he did. He just didn't have all the facts." Sam paused. "Fourteen Japanese girls have actually been kidnapped on Guam in the last year and a half. The first four were taken just over a year ago and were reported as runaways. When the latest girls were taken, nobody went back and asked if there might have been a connection."

"But you found one?"

"Yes. The girls were all taken on Shinto holy days that coincided with spring tides."

"Shinto—that's a Japanese religion, isn't it?"

"Right. That's what tipped me off: the girls were all Japanese. It also explains why those particular girls were taken. Remember what Krauss said? They were all from prominent families, all attending private schools, all in the company of their chaperons? I think the people who took them were trying to increase the odds that the girls were virgins, since only virgins can enter Shinto holy places."

"But they weren't all taken in the spring," Travis said.

"Spring tides have nothing to do with the seasons," Sam said. "Only with the alignment of the sun and moon. The highest tides of the Earth occur when the sun and moon work together."

"So whoever is kidnapping the girls is taking them during high tides. The question is, why?"

Sam shook his head. "That I can't tell you."

Sarah looked confused. "But . . . the girl they found, the dead one." She looked around. "I mean . . . in the autopsy report . . . Well, she wasn't a virgin."

"I know that," Sam said. "I checked. My guess is the kidnappers found out, too, and got rid of her."

"Or deflowered her themselves," Hunter said, "and then dumped her into the ocean."

"My God," Jennifer said. "What kind of animals are they?"

Sam shrugged. "I'm just telling you what I believe. It may not be true. What is true, though, is that the next Shinto holy period is three days long. It's in honor of Amaterasu, the Sun goddess. It starts at midnight tonight and lasts for seventy-two hours, and for those seventy-two hours, the Earth will have the highest tides of the year."

"So, we've got three days to find these guys," Travis said.

"Three days for now," Jack pointed out. "But if we don't find them, we can get them on the next holy day, right?"

Sam shook his head. "That's the problem. This celebration is the last one of the year that occurs during a spring tide. If we don't catch them this time, it'll be months before we can look for them again."

Travis stepped forward and Sam returned to his place by the wall.

"Okay, that's it. I want everyone in place by oh-nine-hundred tomorrow." He looked at Jack. "You going back to your place now?"

"Yeah. Best be on my way."

"Stan? You're checked in downstairs, right?"

"Yep."

"Hunter, where's your room?"

"Upstairs," he said. "In the penthouse."

Travis rubbed the back of his neck. "Blake, you *do* know you're working for the government, right?"

Hunter stood and stretched. "Sure. Working for my dear old rich Uncle Sam." Travis just shook his head.

Sam gave the three men their transceiver arrays and they headed for the door.

"Oh-nine-hundred hours," Travis repeated. "That's when the fun begins."

Chapter Fourteen

Two and a half days later, the fun still hadn't started. Sarah and Jen had been everywhere from hotel row on Tumon Bay to the coral limestone pillars in Latte Park to the open-air market of Chamorro Village without anyone so much as bumping into them. If she'd been on vacation, Sarah might have been enjoying herself. But working under these conditions sucked.

Today was the worst. The salt-tinged ocean breeze they'd enjoyed the first couple of days was gone. In its place was dead air and a sun that burned through the palm trees like a laser. Walking down the sidewalk, looking in the same shops at the same cheap gewgaws, Sarah thought she'd go crazy before the kidnappers made their move. In fact, she almost relished the thought of being abducted. At least then she'd be doing something. Walking around pointlessly, looking in shop windows, trying to decide where to have lunch—how did other women do it?

The disguise, too, was getting old. Taking the latex pieces off three nights in a row had left her fair skin raw, and the hair was so heavy it gave her a headache. The Japanese school uniform was tiresome, too. Why couldn't she wear shorts? Shirt, jumper, sweater, socks—it was like walking around in a cocoon.

"So," Jennifer said. "Where do you want to go now?"

Sarah shrugged. She couldn't say much when there were people around—someone might hear her flawless English and become suspicious.

Jen pointed toward an art gallery down the street. "How about the gallery? We haven't been there since yesterday."

Sarah rolled her eyes and followed Jen down the street.

Of course, it wasn't all bad. Sarah was amused to find that some men took a real interest in her as she was— quiet, sweet, and submissive. It made her wonder if her usually brash and outspoken ways were a bit too up-front for some men. Being raised by hippie parents hadn't given her much polish and the Army didn't waste time teaching their women the feminine arts. It made her wonder if her love life might improve if she hung back and let the guys make the first move once in a while.

That's it. This getup is affecting my brain!

Jennifer wasn't having much more fun than Sarah was, of course; but for the opposite reason. She was used to being stared at, admired, lusted after; and in her frumpy dress and sensible shoes she was somewhat less than stunning. It had to be tough, Sarah thought, giving up all that attention.

The two women finished their pass through the gallery and headed back out onto the sidewalk. Half a block down, Jen stopped.

"God damn it!"

She bent over and took off one of her shoes, shaking a rock out. Sarah knew how she felt. It was the sort of day where any little annoyance could piss you off. Sarah covered her mouth with her hand.

"Sorry."

"Don't be," Jen huffed. "It's just me. I'm getting tired of this shit."

"Yeah, me too."

Two men in business suits passed by and Sarah lowered her gaze. When they'd gone, she glanced back at Jen.

"How much longer have we got?"

Jen checked her watch. "It's four-thirty. Travis said we could take a break at six."

"Too early for dinner, then."

"Yeah."

"How about some shaved ice?"

Jen nodded. "That sounds good."

They walked down the block until they found a vendor. Sarah ordered an orange; Jen's was passion fruit. Sarah took a bite and let the tangy confection melt in her mouth. Okay, so this place wasn't all bad.

As they ate, they continued their stroll.

"God, Jen, I don't know if this is going to work. I mean, we're almost out of time."

"I know what you mean," Jen said. "In two-and-a-half days, nobody's even looked at you and my dogs are killing me."

Sarah stopped. "What's that supposed to mean?"

"My feet hurt."

"No. You said nobody's even looked at me. What are you saying? That I'm not worth looking at?"

Jen sighed. "Don't get all hot about it, okay? All I'm saying is that you haven't been, you know, drawing a lot of attention."

"Oh, and I suppose you have?"

"No. But I'm not supposed to, am I?"

"Besides," Sarah continued, "I've seen plenty of guys looking at me. You just haven't noticed 'cause you've been too busy window shopping."

Jen's cheeks reddened. "Keep your voice down; someone will hear you."

"Fine," Sarah said as she turned and walked briskly away.

"Slow down," Jen said, hurrying to catch up. "You walk like a Marine."

Sarah stopped and glared at her. "I do not walk like a Marine!"

"Shh! You'll blow your cover."

"So what? If I walk like a goddamned Marine, who am I going to fool anyway?"

Jennifer took a deep breath and let it out slowly.

"Okay, let's just stop a second and think about this. We're both tired and stressed out and now we're jumping down each other's throats. I really think we need to just step back from the edge here."

Sarah looked down at her shaved ice. The cup was crushed and most of it had melted and spilled out.

"Sorry. This whole thing's just starting to get to me." She looked up. "I mean, we're running out of time and I can't help thinking that it's my fault."

Jennifer put her hand on Sarah's shoulder. "That's not true. You're doing a great job."

"Even though nobody's looking at me?"

"Well . . . I guess that wasn't entirely true."

"Why'd you say it, then?"

"I don't know. Just jealous I guess."

Sarah's eyes widened. Jen? Jealous of *her*?

"Tell you what," Jen said. "Why don't I ask Travis if we can come in early for dinner? At the pace we're going, it'll take us half an hour to get back to the hotel anyway. I think we've both earned a break."

Sarah smiled. "Sounds good."

Chapter Fifteen

At eighteen hundred hours, they were all back in the hotel room. Jennifer, Travis, and Sarah had already eaten, Stan and Hunter were tucking into some takeout Chinese, and Jack was finishing off a Big Mac. Sam sat by himself, reading a copy of *Wired* magazine.

"Aren't you going to have anything, Sam?" Jen asked.

He shook his head. "I ate before you guys got back."

Travis looked at her. "A bag of Doritos, a package of Mother's cookies, and a Mountain Dew."

"Of course. Salt, sugar, and caffeine: all the major food groups."

"So, what do we do now?" Hunter said.

"Good question." Travis rubbed his forehead. "We've got our hook in the water, but the fish just ain't biting."

"Maybe we've got the wrong bait," Stan said.

Sarah glared at him. "What's that supposed to mean?"

"Anything you want it to mean."

Travis raised his hands. "Things are taking longer than we thought, that's all. It's no big deal."

"Unless midnight rolls around and they still haven't taken her," Stan said. "Then the mission goes down the drain and TALON ends up looking like pussies."

"Watch it," Hunter warned.

"Why should I? I said all along this was a goatfuck. If we screw this up, you think the State Department won't complain about it? Our funding could be gone tomorrow if the word gets around that we're all a bunch of can't cunts."

Travis's face reddened. "Stow it, mister!"

"Sure, I'll stow it," Stan said, pushing his food away. "But when the shit comes down, don't say I didn't warn you." He stood up and stormed into the connecting room. "If anybody wants me, I'll be watching the tube."

The door closed and the six of them looked at one another.

"You think Stan's right?" Jen asked.

Travis shook his head. "I've said all along this is a worthwhile mission. If we can't get it done, nobody can. That's what I'll tell General Krauss if—and I said if— we go home empty-handed."

Jack stood up. "Mind if I head out? I need to get my stuff from the hotel room. Maybe I can look for that dreadlocked white boy on the way."

"Good idea," Travis said.

Jack grabbed his knit cap and left.

"Hunter? Why don't you finish up and get back on the streets? We've still got five hours left. No sense wasting it sitting around here."

"Sure thing."

Travis looked at Sarah.

"I know, I know," she said. "Just give me a second to get the antidote." She headed into the bathroom.

Jen started to put her hair back into a bun. "Man, I hope we get lucky this time," she whispered. "Sarah's about had it."

"I know," Travis said. "Just try to keep her focused. If anybody does try and take her, she needs to be ready."

"God fucking dammit!" It was Stan.

Travis, Jen, Sam, and Hunter charged through the connecting door to see what was wrong.

Stan was standing on the bed, screaming at the television.

"Those assholes! Those fucking motherfuckers!"

"Keep your voice down!" Travis yelled. "What the hell's the matter?"

Stan pointed at the television. "Look! It's on the news."

"What?"

"They took another one," Stan shouted. "They kidnapped another goddamned girl!"

The five of them gathered around and listened to the details. Another Japanese girl had been taken off the streets when her chaperon went to the ladies' room. Same MO. No leads.

Travis sank down on the bed and watched the report. *My God. What are we going to do now?*

The phone rang. He hesitated a moment before picking it up.

"Yes. Hello, sir." He nodded at the others. "We were just watching it on the televis— No, sir. Upset. Yes, sir, I'm sure he would be. Of course. Yes, sir. Good-bye sir."

He hung up and bit the inside of his lip thoughtfully.

"Who was that?"

"General Krauss. He just got a call from the Secretary of State. He wants to know what's going on over here."

"He heard about the other girl already?"

"Apparently so."

"Shit!" Stan slammed his fist into the mattress. "Goddamned REMF's are coming out of the woodwork. TALON is going to take it in the ass for this one!"

Sarah walked into the room and looked at them.

"What's wrong? I could hear Stan from the bathroom."

"That's what's wrong," Stan said, pointing to the television. "While you were out strutting your phony ass all over the streets, the fucking kidnappers took another fucking Japanese girl!"

Sarah's face fell as she looked at the others.

"You guys think this is my fault, don't you?"

"You're goddamned right we do."

"Shut up, Stan!" Travis looked at her. "Nobody's blaming you, Sarah. There are lots of girls out there. We knew there was a possibility—"

"Shit!" Sarah said, stamping her foot. "That's it! I'm tired of this fucking mission and I'm tired of being blamed for every goddamned thing that goes wrong! I didn't want to play dress up in the first place, remember? If the mission goes to hell, it's not my fault!" She turned and stalked into the connecting room.

"Where are you going?" Travis demanded.

"Down to the fucking lobby. I'm going to get myself a candy bar!"

As the door closed, Travis rounded on Stan.

"What the hell did you do that for?"

"What? I didn't say anything."

"Oh, come on Stan," Jen said. "This whole thing's been harder on Sarah than on any of the rest of us. Telling her the problem wasn't her fault wasn't fair."

"Fine," Stan said. "So it's my fault. Well, I did what I was told to do, didn't I? I got us a boat. And I've been on the streets following your sorry asses all over the place for three goddamned days. You think that's fun? Forget it. It fucking stinks!"

"Oh yeah? Try spending three days walking around in the tropics in panty hose—see if *you* like it!"

"All right. That's enough," Travis said. "Stan, go take a walk around the block and cool off. The evening's still young. When Sarah gets back, we'll head out again."

"Why? They've already taken a girl."

"No matter," Travis said. "To quote that famous warrior, Yogi Berra, 'It ain't over 'til it's over.' "

Stan stalked out of the room and slammed the door.

"What's his problem?" Hunter asked.

"Don't worry about it," Travis said. "That's just Stan's way. He's only got two emotions: happy as a pig in shit and totally pissed off. Give him a few minutes and he'll be ready to go out again."

Jen checked her watch. "Well, time's wasting. I'll finish getting ready and go get Sarah."

"Good idea."

She headed back to her room.

Travis sat down and considered what their next move should be. There wasn't enough time left to cover the whole island. They'd just have to pick one spot and go there. But which one?

"Either of you see where that other girl was kidnapped?"

"Apra Heights."

Travis nodded. "Not too close. Good. With the police busy snooping down there, the kidnappers will have to move their operations." He glanced at the connecting door. "Jen?"

"She just left," Hunter said. "I heard her door close."

"When she and Sarah get back, let's have them do the hotel loop again. Hunter, you and Stan take up your usual positions. I'll have Jack tail the girls once he's here." He looked at the takeout cartons on the table. "You want to finish your dinner?"

Hunter shook his head. "Lost my appetite. I'm ready to go any time."

Travis looked at Sam. "How about you?"

"I got another Dewski in the cooler if I need it."

"Okay. Let's get in position."

The lock clicked and the door flew open. Jen was standing in the doorway with a look that was equal parts fear and excitement.

"I can't find Sarah!"

"I thought she was going to the lobby."

"She's not there. I think somebody took her!"

Travis looked at Sam. "Check her signal."

Sam checked the PowerBook. "She's moving!"

"Where?"

"Out of the parking lot. Going fast. She must be in a car." He looked up. "I think they've got her."

Travis let out a whoop. "Let's go get 'em!" He turned. "Hunter, Jen, you two get your suits on and grab your gear. I'll radio Stan and see if he saw anything when Sarah left. Sam?"

"I've already got him."

Travis picked up the microphone. "Stan? Where are you?"

There was a pause and then Stan's voice came through the speakers on the table. "I'm out on Marine Drive. What's up?"

"How far is that from the hotel?"

"A few blocks. Why?"

"The big fish took the bait."

"Holy shit. Where are they now?"

Sam checked the readout. "In a vehicle. Heading south."

"Give me a vector. I'll grab a taxi and follow them."

"Good idea," Travis said. "Hunter and Jen are heading out now; they'll get your gear and meet you there. I'll be there in a few."

Travis turned to Hunter while Sam gave Stan the vector.

"Where'd Jack say he was going?"

"His hotel room," Hunter said. "He was going to get his stuff."

"All right. When Sam's finished, we'll give Jack a call and have him meet Stan. You and Jennifer grab Stan's gear and take off as soon as you're ready. I'll get the rest of the gear together and meet you there as soon as I can."

The bathroom door opened and Jen walked out.

"Bad news." She held out her hand. "I found this in there."

It was Jack's battery array.

Travis slammed his hand into his forehead. "Shit!"

"Don't worry about it," Sam said. "I can still get a message to him."

"Do it. Tell him where Stan's headed and have him meet us there. Hunter? Jen? Get going."

Chapter Sixteen

Jack acquired his target only minutes after leaving the
Hilton. Bopping through the crowd, singing to himself,
the kid was oblivious to the tail as he made his way
toward the seedier side of town. Jack followed at a dis-
creet distance, waiting for the right moment to strike.
He didn't want too many eyewitnesses around when he
asked for his money back.

Luckily, it was a small town—getting to the wrong
side didn't take long. As the crowds thinned and the
streets darkened, Jack put on his knit cap, keeping his
eyes down as he gradually closed the distance between
them. The kid had dropped his dance routine and was
moving smooth as a shark between the rows of tumble-
down apartments. When he made a left into a deserted
street, Jack was on him in a flash.

"Well well," Jack said, grabbing the kid by the neck.
"If it ain't my little white friend. Remember me?"

The white boy blanched so hard the freckles on his
face stood out like zits.

"Hey, bro. What's happen—"

"Cut the crap," Jack snapped, squeezing ever so
slightly harder. He could feel the kid's Adam's apple
jump as he swallowed. "Where are the girls?"

"What girls?"

"The Japanese girls you said you'd take me to,
remember?"

"Oh," the kid said, his voice a strangled sob. "The

girls. Sure. I remember. I said I'd take you there. Musta got high instead. Musta forgot."

"Yeah, you forgot all right. But now you're gonna remember, aren't you?"

"Yeah. I remember real good. Girls. You want girls. Man keeps them down near the marina. I'll take you there. No problem, bro."

Jack released him and the kid staggered back, rubbing the skin of his throat, looking around for anyone who might be able to help him.

Good luck, Jack thought. People in this part of town knew better than to stick their noses into other people's business. He nodded and the two of them headed east.

Five minutes later, the kid stopped in front of a ramshackle house covered with graying clapboard. Weeds grew up through the cracks in the broken-down stoop and the windows were covered with yellowing sheets. The place was only two blocks from the bay. Close enough to smell the rotting fish entrails in the garbage cans behind the restaurants, far enough away that there was no view of the water. Jack noted the deadbolt in the door.

"This the place?"

The kid nodded. "Yeah."

"Who's inside?"

"The girls."

"Who *else,* asshole?"

"Ramon. He makes sure the girls don't leave."

Jack stepped back and did a quick recon of the building. It didn't look like the kind of place where you could hide a bunch of hostages, but you didn't need any brains to be a kidnapper. Maybe the kidnappers moved them around from place to place to keep from arousing suspicion. Still, he'd need some backup before going inside. He reached up behind his ear and stopped.

Shit! He'd left his battery array back in the hotel room.

He looked at the kid. "How many girls are inside?"

"I don't know. Five, six maybe. How many girls you need, man?"

Jack cuffed him on the ear. "None of your god-damned business."

He closed his eyes and assessed the situation. The girls wouldn't put up a fight and the kid was unarmed; but what about this Ramon guy? How many weapons did he have? Was the place booby-trapped? Jack could use the kid as cover, but sooner or later he'd have to disarm whoever was on the other side of the door.

Shit. He needed backup; but if he left to get the others, the girls might be gone when he got back.

When you see the correct course, act; do not wait for orders.

Sun Tzu was right. Jack couldn't wait for the others in order to act. He had to do something now.

"You got a key?"

The kid shook his head. "Ramon's got it locked from inside."

"But he'll open the door if he knows it's you, right?"

"Yeah, bro. He'll open up if I tell him to."

"All right," Jack said. "When I say go, you go up and knock. Tell him you got to get inside—I don't care what excuse you give him. You got that?"

"Sure. Whatever you say, br—"

Jack smacked him on the back of the head. "And stop calling me bro, asshole. I ain't your brother, you shit-faced little pill popper."

The kid nodded.

Jack took the kid by the scruff of his neck and shoved him toward the door.

"All right, now. Let's go inside. And don't make any sudden moves. You give me a hard time, I'll snap your scrawny neck like a twig."

The kid gulped, then stepped forward and knocked on the door. Jack heard footsteps on the other side and a hoarse whisper.

"Who's there?"

Jack's grip tightened on the kid's neck.

"It's me—Donovan. Open the door."

"Donovan? What are you doing here?"

The kid glanced at Jack. "Nothin', man. Nothin'. I just need to come in is all."

"You got the money you owe me?"

Jack nodded.

"Yeah, sure. I got your money. Let me in quick so I don't spend it."

"Okay, man. Hold on."

Jack heard the sound of a bolt being thrown. He raised his foot. As the knob began to turn he kicked in the door and threw the kid in after it.

Jack charged through the open door and crouched, his elbows bent, his hands ready to deliver a blow. Sprawled on the floor in front of him were Donovan and a small, dark-haired man—presumably Ramon. Donovan looked like he'd pissed himself.

Ramon scrambled to his feet. "Who the hell are you?"

"Doesn't matter who I am. Where are the girls?"

"Get outta my house, man. Get out or I'll cut your throat." Ramon pulled out a switchblade and waved it in Jack's direction.

He lunged. Jack sidestepped the blade and grabbed Ramon's wrist, twisting the man's arm until the knife fell to the floor. Then kept twisting. Ramon's legs crumpled and he went down on one knee. Jack leaned over and put his face in Ramon's.

"Where . . . are . . . the girls?"

Ramon pointed a shaky finger toward a door on the far wall.

"In there, man. Go ahead, take 'em. They're yours."

Jack grabbed Ramon's shirt and pulled him to his feet. "Do I look that stupid, dickhead? You go first."

He shoved Ramon toward the door and picked up the knife. The man just stood there.

"Go on," Jack yelled. "Open the goddamned door!"

Ramon swallowed. "I don't know if they're ready or not."

"I don't fucking care if they're ready!" Jack put his foot in Ramon's back and shoved. "Open the fucking door!"

Jack tensed, the knife in his hand, ready for an assault. Ramon opened the door. Nothing happened.

"You want 'em? There they are."

Jack stepped forward and shoved Ramon aside. It was

dark in the room. He reached around and flipped the switch.

There were five of them—huddled together, sitting on a pair of stained mattresses—clinging to one another in fright. Five little girls in lace panties and high heels, their young faces painted like cheap whores. The oldest one was maybe nine. Jack crossed to a closet on the far side of the room, secured it, and went back into the front room where Ramon and Donovan stood like burglars caught by a security camera.

"Who else is in here?" he demanded.

"Nobody. Honest," Ramon said. He looked at Donovan and the two of them nodded.

Jack checked the rest of the place out. There was a bathroom in the back and a tiny refrigerator in the kitchen; except for that, all the place had in it was Ramon's easy chair, a bunch of trash, and a hot plate.

When he was satisfied the place was secure, Jack went back to where Donovan and Ramon were standing.

"Who are those girls?"

Ramon had gotten brave in the last few minutes. He puffed himself up and gave Jack a cocky nod.

"They're mine," he said. He had a gold front tooth and a lot of hair sticking out of his ears and nose. He reeked of tobacco and body odor.

"What do you mean, they're 'yours'?"

"I own them," Ramon said. "Paid good money, too." He smirked. "You want one, it'll cost you a thousand dollars—cash."

Jack could feel his face darken. This guy was nothing but a goddamned slave trader! Selling little girls like they were pieces of meat. He looked at Donovan the ganja-head, nodding and grinning like it was all some kind of joke, and the rage boiled up inside of him.

The first blow wiped the smile off Ramon's ugly face. The second took his gold tooth with it. Seeing his friend go down, Donovan turned and ran for the door. He didn't make it. Jack swung his leg in a low arc and cut the kid's feet out from under him. Then he pulled him to his feet.

"Where are their parents?"

The kid's hands were up, protecting his face. "I don't know, man. I—"

Jack punched him in the stomach. The kid doubled over, staggered, and puked on the floor. Jack grabbed his shirt and shook him.

"I asked you where their parents were, asshole. I'm not going to ask nicely again."

"Don't hurt me," the kid whimpered. "Please. I didn't take them. Ramon did."

Jack shoved him backward and he crumpled on the floor.

"I only find the customers for him. Honest. Don't kill me."

Jack sneered. "If I was going to kill you, I'd have done it already."

He stepped across the room and kicked Ramon in the side. No response. The guy was out cold.

Jack walked back into the bedroom.

"Any of you speak English in here?"

One little girl raised her hand.

Jack bent down on one knee. "What's your name, honey?"

"Lita."

The girl was shivering. Jack took his shirt off and put it on over her head.

"Lita, how old are you?"

"Six."

Jack closed his eyes and reconsidered killing Ramon.

"Lita, where are your parents?"

Tears welled up in the girl's eyes. "I don't know. I, I just—"

She burst into tears and fell into Jack's arms. He patted her back.

"Jack! Jack, can you hear me? Over."

Jack reached for the transmitter behind his ear and stopped. He'd left his battery array back at the Hilton. What was this all about?

"Jack, this is Sam. They took Sarah! Repeat. Sarah is on the move. I know you can't talk to me, but if you can hear this get down to Apra Harbor, north end. Stan's there now, waiting for Hunter and Jen." He gave

Jack the address. "I'll repeat this message every couple of minutes until they tell me you're there. If you don't show up in ten minutes, Hunter will come looking for you. They've got her, Jack! Go get 'em. Over."

Jack looked at the little girl in his arms. He couldn't just leave her here, could he? But Sarah was in danger and he had a job to do.

What was he going to do?

"Is there a phone in here?" he asked.

Lita shook her head. "No phone here." She pointed to the wall.

Jack wiped a hand down his face. Shit. Now what?

Lita wriggled out of his arms and walked toward the door.

"Don't go out there," Jack said, wanting to spare her the sight of two bloodied men.

Lita peeked out the door and saw Ramon, lying on the ground, face down.

"Phone there," she said, pointing at him.

Jack's eyebrows shot up. "A cell phone?"

The girl nodded.

Jack stepped out and frisked Ramon, pulling the cell phone from his back pocket. He dialed 9-1-1.

"Hello, operator? Yeah, I've got some little girls here who need your help."

Chapter Seventeen

Apra Harbor was a natural lagoon on Guam's southwest coastline, the biggest commercial port on the island. Stan glanced back down the road—past the Port Authority building, the fuel pier, and the dry dock where ships from all over the South Pacific came to be repaired—looking for Travis. Still no sign of him. He crouched lower in the shadows and returned his attention to the building where Sarah had been taken.

It was a four-story warehouse, with a six foot wide wooden walkway that ran around the perimeter. The place was on the farthest north point of Apra Harbor, surrounded by sand and beach grass and driftwood. There were no lights on outside the building, but several lights burned inside. Stan had gotten there too late to see Sarah go inside, but he'd been monitoring her signal with the receiver Hunter brought him. This was the place they'd taken her all right—no doubt about that.

Hunter and Jen were covering the far side. They were already in their suites; Stan had his weapon and his helmet.

"Any sign of Travis? Over." It was Jen.

Stan reached up and pressed his transmitter. "Negative. You guys see anything on that side?"

"No. Nothing through the thermal viewer, either. My guess is they're in a room near the middle of the building. You still picking up Sarah's signal? Over."

Stan looked down at the portable receiver that Sam had made before leaving Maui.

"Affirmative. What do you hear from C and C? Over."

"Travis is on his way. Sam's still trying to get hold of Jack. Over."

Stan looked around. "He must not be close. We would have seen him by now. Let me know if you see anything over there. Out."

Stan hunkered down and propped his Squad Automatic Weapon on its bipod. Waiting was always the hardest part. Holding still, being quiet, keeping watch made Stan feel like he was going to bust out of his skin. Giving a SEAL a mission and telling him to wait was like giving Jeff Gordon a can of gas and telling him to pour it on the ground.

He checked his watch: Nineteen-oh-two. How much longer were they going to let these guys keep Sarah in there? If they were the nuts Travis said they were, they could be doing anything to her. The back of his eyeballs itched. He wanted to kill something.

Then Sarah's signal stopped. Stan tapped the receiver. Nothing.

"Hunter! Jen! I lost Sarah!"

"What do you mean you lost her?"

"Her signal. I was looking at the monitor and everything was fine and the next thing I knew it was gone."

"Hold on. Hunter's talking to Sam. Over."

Stan stood and looked at the warehouse. Nobody at the windows. What the hell was happening?

"Stan? Sam's lost her, too. What'll we do? Over."

"Go in and get her."

"Without Travis?"

"Yes, dammit! This is my call. Hunter, get your butt over here and help me make the charge. Jen, stay where you are and cover the back door. Don't announce your presence. Once Hunter and I are inside, we'll send for you. Ready?"

Stan saw sand fly as Hunter came scrambling toward him.

"Ready," said Jen.

"On my mark, then. Go!"

Stan and Hunter ran for the door. Just as in the drill

on Maui, Stan kicked the door in and Hunter went first, his rifle at the ready. There was no grenade flash, no smart rifle, but the tactics were the same: get inside, find the hostages, and get rid of the bogeys.

Inside the building was a room with a formica counter, a couple of fake plants, and a few chairs scattered around. A door leading into the back was on the right. Stan pressed his transmit button and whispered to Jen.

"We're inside. No Sarah. Anything out there? Over."

"Negative. Want me to come around?"

"Not yet. Keep your eyes open. I'll call you. Out."

Stan looked at Hunter and indicated the door. Hunter nodded. Stan crouched down and pushed the door open with his shoulder, his rifle at the ready.

The door led into a long hallway with doors coming off it on either side and an exit sign over a blue door at the end. The doors were closed. No one in sight. Stan motioned to Hunter and the two of them ran down the hall.

The first office door had a window in it. With Hunter covering him, Stan crept up the wall and peered inside. Nobody there. He looked at Hunter and shook his head.

They went to the next door. No one in that office, either. Stan looked around. Time was running out. They needed more manpower.

He reached up behind his ear. "Jen, this is Stan. Still no Sarah. We're going to split up and search this place. Anything out there? Over."

"Jack just showed up. He's putting on his suit."

"Forget the suit. Get in here. Enter through the first door. We're twenty feet down the hallway on your right."

"We're on our way. Out."

Stan sank down on his haunches and checked his watch. They'd lost Sarah's signal five minutes and twelve seconds ago. If her heart had stopped then— and she wasn't too badly injured—they could still revive her; but they didn't have long. He heard Jack and

Jen enter the building and watched as they scrabbled down the hallway toward his position. Jack was drenched in sweat; he wasn't wearing a shirt.

"Jen says you lost Sarah's signal."

Stan nodded. "Five minutes ago."

"Could it be an implant malfunction?"

"Let's find her first. We can figure out what went wrong later." He turned. "Hunter? You and Jen check upstairs. Jack and I will take the first floor. If you see anything, holler."

"Got it."

The two of them ran to the stairwell door and charged inside.

Stan turned to Jack. "Let's split up and see what's in the rest of these offices."

Jen clambered up the stairwell, her rifle in her hand. At the top of the steps, Hunter crouched beside the door and she peered through the window.

"All clear."

"Okay. Let's go."

He opened the door and the two of them charged through.

This floor also consisted of a hallway that ran along the building's flank, right to left, with doors coming off either side. Jen looked at the heather gray carpet, the overhead lighting, the drinking fountain, and the two red fire extinguishers.

"Something's not right."

Hunter looked at the same things and shook his head. "What's not right about it? It looks like a million other office buildings."

"That's what's bothering me."

He shook his head. "Let's split up. We can cover more ground that way. I'll go right, you go left."

Hunter hoisted his M-16 and hurried down the hall to the right. Jen shouldered her own weapon and ran for the first door on her left.

She checked the first two rooms quickly and moved on. Something about the place was giving her the creeps. No kidnappers, no hostages; but no one else, either. She ran to the third office and opened the door. The place seemed almost eerily familiar. What was it about this place that gave her the creeps?

She stepped out of the last office and turned. Hunter had just checked out his last door, too. She pressed her transmitter and whispered.

"Anything?"

He shook his head.

She pressed again. "Stan? Second floor is all clear. How's it going down there? Over."

"Nothing but empty offices."

"How long has it been?"

There was a pause. "Seven minutes."

"Shit." Seven minutes was long enough for brain damage to occur. If Sarah's heart had stopped, she might be too far gone to revive. Jen swallowed the lump in her throat.

"Hunter and I are heading up to the third floor. I'll call you when we get there."

"Do it. Out."

Hunter ran back into the stairwell and Jen followed him up. Their boots clanged on the metal steps as they bolted to the top.

What was it about this place that was bothering her? From the outside, it looked like a warehouse. But inside it was just row after row of offices, each one nearly identical to the one before. It reminded Jen of something. Something she couldn't quite put her finger on.

Hunter reached the landing and grabbed the door handle.

"I think we hit pay dirt." He pointed to the door. "It's locked; and it's the first one without a window. This must be the place." He pressed his transmitter. "Stan? This is Hunter. I think we've got something. Over."

"Did you find Sarah?"

"No. But this is the first locked door we've come to—that's suspicious enough. I'm going in."

"Jack and I are heading up. Out."

Hunter looked at Jen. She crouched, her weapon at the ready. He slung his weapon, took a step back, lifted his leg, and slammed his foot into the door.

Chapter Eighteen

August 21, 1912 hours,
a warehouse at Apra Harbor, Guam

"Help! Stan, Jack, help me!"

Jennifer's scream raised the hair on Stan's neck. He and Jack charged up the stairs, taking them three at a time.

"Hurry!"

Jack surged ahead with Stan hot on his heels. As they rounded the last bend in the metal stairs, Stan saw Jennifer through the slats, flat on her stomach, leaning through the open door. Beyond the door was nothing but black.

"What the hell?"

Hunter was dangling over the precipice where the third floor should have been. Jennifer was holding his foot.

"Help me pull him up!" she yelled. "I can't hold him much longer!"

Jack went down on his belly and grabbed Hunter's other leg, Stan grabbed Jack's feet, and the three of them pulled Hunter from the abyss. When he was safely on the landing, Stan leaned over and looked out. The door had opened out into a vast black emptiness.

"What happened?"

Hunter was rubbing his ankle. "I kicked the door and lost my balance. The next thing I knew I was falling. Thank God Jen grabbed my foot."

Jennifer shook her head. "If you guys hadn't gotten here in time, he might have gone all the way down."

"Yeah," Jack said, peering into the darkness, "but all the way down into what?"

"Now I know why this place gives me the creeps," Jennifer gasped. "It's like a movie set."

"Huh?"

She looked at Stan. "You know, like a back lot or a soundstage in Hollywood. It's got just enough in it to fool the audience and make them think that what they're seeing is real. A sound stage can look like a regular house, but if you see it from another angle, you can tell it's fake."

"So what we're doing here is seeing this place from the other angle?"

"Exactly."

"But those offices were real," Hunter said.

She shook her head. "They *seemed* real; but I'll bet if we'd pulled out a drawer or tried to turn on a computer, nothing would have worked. There aren't any air vents, either. Did you notice? It's the same way with this whole building. From the outside, it looks like a warehouse; but inside it's full of nothing."

"Yeah. I noticed that," Stan said. "But it doesn't help us find Sarah."

"Yes, it does," Jen said. "Now that we're onto them, they can't fool us anymore. We know this place isn't a warehouse, we know it's not an office building. All we have to find out is what it *is*."

"All right. Let's have another look." Stan flipped down his visor and stuck his head through the door.

It was a cavernous area, maybe half a football field across. The perimeter walls were covered with catwalks that stretched between connecting ladders, but the ground was hard to make out. He checked the thermal viewer.

"No bogeys inside."

"How about Sarah?"

"Nope."

"Then where is she?" Jen asked.

"I don't know," Stan said. "But I do know how to get through this door." He stepped up to the threshold and slid his left foot in a half circle around to the right, holding the wall as he searched the ground with his toe.

"Be careful," Jennifer said. "You'll fall."

"No, I won't." Stan felt something solid under his foot. "There's a platform here and a ladder underneath." He turned. "Hunter? You follow me. Jen, Jack, you follow Hunter." He turned and stepped through the door.

The four of them made their way down the first ladder to a connecting catwalk and from there to another ladder that led deeper into the body of the building. Every step of the way, Stan searched the ground below. He didn't see Sarah, but what he smelled bothered him.

It was sea water.

He'd noticed it as soon as they stepped onto the first catwalk: the unmistakable smell of the ocean. And now, as they got closer to the bottom, he heard water lapping against concrete. He was beginning to get the picture, and he didn't like it.

When they reached the ground, they did a quick recon of the area and found no sign of anyone. Thermal viewers weren't as good as Night Vision Goggles, though, and Stan didn't feel 100 percent sure that there wasn't a bogey lurking behind something. He began searching for a way to turn on a light.

Twenty feet away, Stan found what looked like a main power switch on the wall. He hesitated. If he threw the switch and the lights came on, they'd be easy targets for anyone with a weapon and good aim. But time was wasting. Sarah had been off the screen for fifteen minutes, and every second that ticked by was another chance they'd never find her. He wished Travis were there with the NVGs. He wished he'd never lost Sarah in the first place. Most of all, he wished the goddamned unfriendlies would show up so he could kill somebody.

He motioned for the others to get down and threw the switch. There was a hum and a click and the overhead lights came on dimly.

"What's wrong?" he whispered.

"Nothing," Hunter said. "They're high pressure sodium. It takes awhile for them to come on."

Stan nodded and looked around as the lights slowly came up, trying to make something out of the soft gray shapes all around him.

When he could finally make something out, it hit him like a blow to the gut. Stan stepped forward and looked at the concrete perimeter, the metal railing embedded in it, and most especially the corrugated metal platform that jutted out over the water from the top of a short flight of stairs.

Jennifer flipped up her visor. "It looks like a giant swimming pool."

Stan took his helmet off. "It's not a swimming pool," he said. "It's a sub dock."

"A *what*?"

"A submarine dock," Stan said, pointing. "They put this building up next to the water and dug the damned thing out underneath. That's why they needed a high tide. The sub needed the extra depth to get out into the harbor."

"That's also why we lost her signal," Hunter said. "When they closed the hatch, it was cut off."

"Fuck!" Stan slammed his hand against the metal railing. "They took her away in a goddamned sub!"

"Oh, shit."

"Oh shit is right."

Jen opened her mouth. "Hold on. I'm getting something." She listened, then placed her finger behind her ear. "Got it." She looked at Stan. "Travis is outside. He wants to know what's going on."

Chapter Nineteen

Sam stood at his console in the Hilton, waiting to hear from Travis. It had been almost forty minutes since he'd lost Sarah's signal and he was frantic with worry. Had the implant failed? Had it been destroyed? Worse yet, was Sarah dead? Sam knew the implant was okay—he'd just checked it out that morning—and if it had been destroyed, that would have to mean Sarah's captors had discovered it. That left only the unthinkable. He closed his eyes and said a prayer.

"Sam? This is Travis. We've got a problem down here. Over."

Sam pressed the transmit button on his console. "What's going on, Boss? Everything's been garbled. Did you find Sarah?"

"Yes and no. We think they've got her in a sub. Would that account for the loss of signal?"

A submarine! Holy shit.

Sam nodded. "Yeah. Her signal's not strong enough to transmit through a solid metal hull; and even if it were, nothing can get through water." He paused. "What are we going to do?"

"Good question. Stan's gone to the naval base to get the Mark Five; Hunter and Jack are heading out in a minute to get the plane. I figure we'll just get out there and start looking for them."

"Don't do that," Sam said. "It's a waste of time. Unless he surfaces, you're never going to find him."

"I'm all ears if you've got a better idea."

Sam rubbed his chin. "How about if I tie into SOSUS? They monitor all the traffic in this area. If I can't find your sub, I can at least narrow down the search. Over."

"You're a genius, Sam. How long will it take to get SOSUS on the line?"

"I'm not sure. Even a genius has to wait for the proper clearances."

"I can help you with that. Get your request ready and I'll be there in a few minutes. Travis out."

2010 hours

Sam had his request ready when the three of them entered the hotel room. Travis threw his gear on the bed and walked over to the console.

"How's it going?"

"Got all my i's dotted and my t's crossed. Where's Jen?"

"Back at the dock, waiting for Stan. I told her to check in when he gets there. You haven't submitted the request yet, have you?"

"No."

"Good. I need a secure line out."

Sam pointed to the phone. "Already taken care of. Once you're past the switchboard, everything going out is scrambled."

"Must be nice being a mind reader."

"I like to think of it as employment insurance."

Travis picked up the phone and dialed General Krauss. Krauss picked up on the second ring.

"General? Major Barrett here. I'm about to submit a request for SOSUS access." He looked at Sam and nodded. "Uh-huh. It's going to need highest priority. Right. Thanks, General, I— No. No, everything's fine. I'll let you know. All right."

Travis hung up. "He says to give him five minutes. After that, SOSUS is all yours."

"Thanks." Sam sat down at his console.

"How come nobody at the naval base heard this sub?"

Hunter asked. "They're tied into SOSUS. You'd think they'd have picked him up."

Sam shook his head. "Too much background noise close to shore. SOSUS won't even pick him up until he's at least a couple of miles out."

"What if he never gets that far away?" Jack asked.

"He will," Travis said. "What's the point of taking a sub if you're not planning on a long haul?"

"And if you're in a hurry," Sam added, "there's no point in taking a sub, either. Stan's Mark Five could run rings around a sub and still beat him to his destination. The point isn't speed, it's stealth. That's why we need SOSUS. It'll tell us this guy's secrets."

Travis checked his watch. "Five minutes. Let's see if Krauss is as good as his word."

Sam submitted his request and waited. Jack and Hunter stepped forward and the four of them stared at the screen.

"Nothing's happening," Jack said.

Travis frowned. "Don't worry. It will."

"It always takes a few minutes," said Sam.

The minutes ticked by.

"What's the holdup?"

"Maybe the satellite link's the problem."

"No. I don't think it's—"

The screen flashed, and the entry screen for the underwater SOund SUrveillance System came up.

Jack let out a whoop and raised his fists in the air. "Thank you, Jesus!"

Travis gave Hunter a high five.

Sam tried hard to suppress a grin. He cracked his fingers dramatically and wiggled them over the keyboard.

"Stand back, gentlemen," he said, "and prepare to be amazed."

Chapter Twenty

They put the girls in the crew's quarters. Two to a bunk, they were crammed in like sardines at the end of the long, narrow room. Sarah lay on her side, her back to the bulkhead, the engine's vibrations tormenting the muscles in her shoulders and back. How long had they been in here? she wondered. An hour, at least—maybe more. The other girls were quiet. A couple had cried themselves to sleep, the others lay in stunned silence as the sub continued toward its destination.

Sarah went over the abduction in her head for the hundredth time. They'd grabbed her by the ice machine—two burly Japanese men who'd thrown a blanket over her head and stuffed her into a laundry cart. She could easily have gotten away; but the team had been waiting three days for something to happen. She couldn't just blow the mission because the timing was bad.

Damn! If she hadn't run off like she did, she'd have had Jen with her when she was taken and she'd know the team was on her trail. Now she wasn't so sure. The getaway from the hotel had been so fast. How long before the team had even realized she was gone?

Sarah shifted her weight, trying to relieve some of the pressure on her shoulder. At least the news wasn't all bad, she thought. At least she had the antidote.

She also had her hands free—or at least as good as. Houdini's rope trick had worked. By flexing her wrists and holding her hands slightly apart while they were tied, she'd been able to create enough slack in the rope to pull her hands out once the time was right. Until then, though, she was leaving them where they were. If she took her hands out too soon and got caught, she might not be able to do the trick a second time.

Sarah lifted her head and looked around at the faces in the other bunks. Was one of these girls the ambassador's niece? She hoped so. Even if they managed to get the girls out alive, if the team didn't produce Aiyako, it'd be hard to call the mission a success. She bent her arm and rested on her elbow.

"Aiyako?" she whispered. None of the girls stirred. Sarah squinted. In the low light, it was hard to see the other faces clearly.

"Aiyako?" she said a little louder.

A girl in the opposite bunk opened her eyes and mumbled something. It was Aiyako; Sarah recognized her from her picture.

Sarah tried to think of what to say. The only words Sam had taught her were simple phrases—not nearly enough to carry on a conversation. But Aiyako was a well-educated young woman. Her English was probably a lot better than Sarah's Japanese. She decided to take a chance.

"Do you speak English?"

The girl nodded. "I know a little."

"Good," Sarah said, greatly relieved.

Another girl in the bunk at Sarah's feet whispered. "Who are you?"

Sarah looked at her. "You speak English, too?"

"We all do," another whispered.

Sarah chuckled, feeling foolish. *Well, what did you expect?*

The girl at Sarah's feet sat up. "You will help us?"

"I will if I can."

The girl looked disappointed.

"Don't worry," Sarah said. "I work for the United States government. There are others with me."

Aiyako gasped. "Inside ship?"

Sarah shook her head. "No. But don't worry, they're coming."

A third girl whispered something to Aiyako, who answered in soothing tones.

"What's the matter?" Sarah asked.

"Gia say we should not talk. I tell her no worry."

Sarah looked toward the empty bunks at the end of the room. The crewmen were all at their stations for now, but it wouldn't be long before they came back. If she was going to find out anything about the men who'd taken them, she'd have to ask now.

"Listen, do any of you know why these guys kidnapped us?"

The girls looked around, shaking their heads and questioning each other in Japanese. Only Aiyako sat strangely silent amidst the banter. Sarah's eyes narrowed. Why was Aiyako reluctant to say anything? Was it because of the others? Or because she didn't trust Sarah?

After another minute, the girls quieted down and Aiyako spoke for the group.

"We know nothing," she said.

Chapter Twenty-one

When the SOSUS data came in, it wasn't the flood of information that Travis had been expecting. It was more like a trickle. Jen radioed to tell him that Stan had arrived with the Mark V and Travis sent them to get supplies. Jack and Hunter were putting their gear together and rechecking their weapons in the other room. Only Sam remained where he had been for the last forty minutes: hunkered over the computer with his headphones on, comparing screw noises with subs known to be in the area, and trying to figure out which of the hundreds of blips on the screen was their man. Finally, he reached out and touched the screen.

"I've got him."

"All right." Travis pulled his chair in closer.

"But there's a problem." Sam leaned back and stretched, rubbing his eyes with the palms of his hands.

Travis's patience was thin. "What kind of problem?"

Sam sighed and dropped his hands. "I'm only picking him up intermittently; he's moved into an area where some of SOSUS's lines are down."

"You mean you can't track him?"

"Not as well as I thought I could, no."

Jack and Hunter had come into the room when they heard Sam's announcement.

"What's the matter? Isn't it going to work?"

"I didn't say that," Sam said irritably. "It's just going to take some more tweaking, that's all."

Travis nodded. "Okay. What do you need to tweak it?"

Sam scratched his head. "Something to fill in the blanks."

"Like what?"

"A sonar array. Maybe a sonobuoy."

"I can get one of those at the naval station. What do we do then?"

"Drop it into the water so I can triangulate the sub's position. That's the problem. We need a helicopter to drop it from and we don't have one."

"Can't we drop it from the Lear?"

Hunter shook his head. "Even if I could go in slow enough, the Lear can't drop anything in flight. The cabin's pressurized."

Sam nodded. "And I'll need more than one reading."

Travis thought for a moment. Anderson Air Force Base was only a short drive away. He could call the base commander and request an Iroquois. But did that violate Krauss's directive not to reveal their operation to the locals? And even if it didn't, that still left the problem of time. No matter how much pressure came from the top, it'd still take at least a day to ready a piece of equipment like a chopper. By the time an Iroquois could be made available and checked out by its crew, the kidnappers could have Sarah and the girls halfway across the Pacific.

"I suppose I could get us a chopper up at Anderson," he said, "but it'll take some time. I don't know what kind of range it has, either . . ."

"Don't do that," Hunter said. "I've got a better idea."

Chapter Twenty-two

Brad LeRoy was already in his pajamas when the two men showed up on his doorstep. He peered out his window at Hunter and Jack and gave them a curious smile. Hunter waved and pointed at the handle, trying to pantomime opening the door. Brad opened it cautiously.

"Red?"

"Hi, Brad. Listen, I need to talk to you about the Goose."

The older man scratched his head. "Don't tell me you want to take her out *now*."

"I want to do more than that," Hunter said. "I want to buy her."

LeRoy's eyebrows shot up. "*Buy* her? Son, you haven't even flown her yet."

"Don't need to. Not if I've got your word that she's in good shape."

"She's in good shape *for an old plane*. But can't we do this tomorrow? I've got to get some shuteye."

"No, sir. This is urgent."

LeRoy's eyes narrowed. "This doesn't have anything to do with drugs, does it?"

Hunter didn't have time to argue; they were running out of time. Brad LeRoy seemed like a guy who knew how to keep his mouth shut. He decided to take a chance.

"This can't go any farther, you understand?"

LeRoy nodded.

"Your country needs your help." Hunter reached into his pocket and grabbed a wad of hundred dollar bills.

"I'm prepared to give you five thousand dollars in cash right now, and the balance in two days."

Brad LeRoy's eyes widened at the sight of the money. "Is this legal?"

"As legal as the government that printed these."

The older man glanced at Jack, doing a quick survey of his massive build. "He's part of this, too?"

"Yes, sir."

"Mind if I ask what you need it for?"

Hunter grinned. "We're huntin' subs."

LeRoy considered another few seconds, then nodded his head. "All right, she's yours. Just give me a second to put on my pants."

2245 hours, Guam International Airport

Half an hour later, Hunter was standing on the tarmac outside the hangar. A faint light still glowed on the western horizon, but the sky overhead was filled with stars. The Grumman Goose idled nearby, its lights on and its wheels chocked, the old crate buzzing like a dragonfly. The sonobuoy had been loaded in the front, ready to drop. Jack brought their weapons up from the car.

"Where do I put these?"

"In the back, behind the toolbox."

"The *toolbox*?"

"It came with the plane. Don't worry, everything's fine."

Jack stepped into the plane just as Brad LeRoy came out of the hangar. He was pushing a maintenance cart, a tarp draped over its top.

"You said you were going sub hunting," he yelled over the drone of the engines, "so I brought you these!"

Hunter looked at the cart. "What are they?"

"Hedgehogs!"

"You're kidding!" Hedgehog was the nickname given to the Mk 10 & 11 antisubmarine grenades used in World War II. Unlike depth charges, hedgehogs didn't explode unless they hit something metal. You could drop one in the water and not worry about scaring off your target with a missed shot.

LeRoy threw back the tarp. "We can put them in the passenger area. When you find your sub, just arm one and push her overboard."

Hunter looked at the yard-long, bottle-shaped projectiles. "Are you sure they still work?"

"Positive."

Hunter clapped him on the back. "You're an ace, Brad."

He called Jack out of the plane and the old man showed them how to arm the fuse. Then they loaded the hedgehogs into the Goose and Jack got back into his seat.

Brad shook Hunter's hand. "Take good care of her, Red. Or whatever your name is."

"Thank you, sir. I will."

He climbed into the cockpit. Jack had the light on and was studying the map. Hunter grabbed the wheel and Brad unchocked the tires. It felt great to be flying a real plane—one that required some skill—for a change. He looked at Jack and smiled.

"You ready?"

"As ready as I'll ever be."

Hunter called the tower and got the go-ahead. He pushed the throttle forward, moving it slowly out toward the runway, and glanced back at Brad LeRoy standing under a spotlight in a pair of coveralls. He gave him a thumbs-up. The older man waved and returned the sign.

The tower cleared him for take-off. Hunter turned the amphib's nose into the wind and checked the plane's gauges one more time. All systems were go. He pushed the throttle forward and the engines roared.

"All right! Let's see what this bird can do!"

The plane surged forward, picking up speed as she headed down the runway. The engines' roar was deafening. Hunter's teeth chattered as the plane's vibrations increased and the lights of the city rushed past her shuddering windows.

"Come on, baby."

The plane went faster, its wheels hopping ever so slightly as it continued its drive down the runway.

"Do it, baby," Hunter coaxed. "Come on!"

They should be in the air by now. He passed the tower. Still on the ground. Hunter opened it up to full throttle and eased the wheel back just a notch to increase the lift.

"Do it for me!"

And then they were up. The plane broke free of the ground and rose like a bird.

"Awesome!" Hunter banked the plane out over the water as it continued its climb. No more bus driving for him.

When they reached cruising altitude, he hailed Travis.

"This is Blake. I'm in the air and I need a vector. Over."

"Sam's getting that for you now. What's all the noise coming from? Over."

"The plane. The vibrations are hellacious, but she's just what we need for a sea hunt. We've got the sonobuoy on board and I got a couple of hedgehogs, too, in case we need to coax our sub to the surface. Over."

"Hedgehogs, huh? Good work. We're going to need all the help we can get."

"My thoughts exactly. How long's it been?"

"Almost four hours since we lost the signal."

"They still submerged?"

"As far as we can tell. Sam's got your vector for you now. Let us know when you're in position so we can get those readings."

"Roger. I'll stay in touch. Out."

Chapter Twenty-three

Stan paced the dock, eager to get underway as Travis and Sam secured Sam's PowerBook to the Mark V's console. Team Five would be pissed when they found out he'd drilled holes in their precious plaything, but there wasn't much choice. Shit, nothing a little Bondo wouldn't take care of. To find the sub, they needed Sam; and Sam needed his computer. If they hit some rough seas, they couldn't afford to have their link to SOSUS go overboard.

One good thing: the Mark V was everything Gus had said it was and then some. Even with the extra fuel weight, the craft rode high in the water, cutting through the waves effortlessly. If it hadn't been so much fun, the push-up contest would have been worth it just to have an excuse to drive this boat. Stan had taken a few practice runs through the harbor while he and Jen waited for Travis and Sam to arrive. The feel of the ocean churning under his feet wasn't sex, but it sure was the next best thing.

Unfortunately, though, the Mark V was built for speed, not comfort. If the team had to follow their sub much more than a couple hundred miles, they'd be pulverized by the time they got there. Stan watched as Sam hooked his computer up to the Mark V's electrical system. Where the hell were they going? he wondered.

"We can shove off any time," Travis said.

Stan untied the belaying lines. Jennifer was standing in the bow in her wetsuit; he jumped in next to her.

"Whoa, you paint that thing on yourself?" he asked, leering. "Maybe next time I could give you some help."

"Sure thing baby," she purred. "I'll bet you're a regular Prickcasso."

Stan howled with laughter as he took his seat at the console. Travis and Jen exchange high fives.

Sam was busy monitoring the SOSUS output. Stan started up the boat and glanced at the screen.

"How far are we from the target?"

"Almost seventy miles," Sam said. "He's doing about fifteen knots. Once Hunter drops the sonobuoy, I can give you a proper vector. Until then, just keep to a north by northwest heading."

"That puts us on top of him in just over an hour." He turned to Travis. "I don't think we ought to shadow the guy. If he thinks we're looking for him, he may not come up. And if he comes up and sees us, he might go down and stay down."

"I agree. We don't want to give him the heebie-jeebies." Travis looked at Sam. "Any luck yet with that program?"

Sam shook his head.

"What program?"

"Sam's running a check of the SOSUS database to see if he can find out where our sub's gone in the past. If we can find a pattern, we may be able to leapfrog him and beat him to the punch."

"Every sub's got a signature sound," Sam said. "From the screw noises, I'd say this guy's a Z V class ballistic missile sub."

"That's an old Soviet sub," Stan said. "A diesel, not a nuke."

"That's right, but your answer was not in question form. The SOSUS records will tell us if the same type of sub was in these waters in the last six months, and if so what his destination was."

Stan nodded. "Good idea. Let me know when you've got your answer. In the meantime . . ." He maneuvered past the last ship in the harbor and out into the open water. "Hold on, everybody. I got the need for speed!"

Chapter Twenty-four

August 22, 0001 hours,
somewhere over the South Pacific

"Sam! Can you hear me?" Hunter strained to hear over the engine noise. "We're in position now. When do you want us to drop this thing? Over."

Sam's voice was clear and calm. "Give me your coordinates. Over."

Hunter gave him the reading from his GPS.

"Put her down right there and have Jack lower the sonobuoy. As soon as I get a reading, you can pick her up and go to the next triangulation point."

"Roger."

Hunter set the plane down in the dark water, his spotlight finding a trough to put her in. Jack opened his door just as a wave hit and salt water sprayed into the cockpit. The sonobuoy went over the side and landed with a splash.

"It's in the water," Hunter said. "Let me know when you've got your reading."

The two of them sat quietly as the plane bobbed on the black water, riding the waves like the ungainly goose it was named for. Hunter kept a steady pressure on the throttle to keep the engines from dying. The last thing he wanted was to have to do a restart in the water.

He turned to Jack.

"You okay? With the plane, I mean."

Jack shrugged. "Not exactly the Concorde, is it?"

Hunter shook his head. Jack knew that he had, in fact, flown the Concorde before. What Jack didn't know was that Hunter actually preferred the Goose.

He heard Sam's voice in his ear.

"I've got the signal. Mark that. You can take her out now."

Jack nodded, pulled the buoy from the water, and closed the door.

"Man, it sure is cold for the tropics."

"It's always cold over the water." Hunter pressed his transmitter. "Where to now? Over."

Sam gave him the new coordinates. "Tell me when you get there. I'll be waiting. Out."

Hunter pushed the throttle forward and the plane took off again. He'd never flown a Grumman Goose before; he wondered how she'd gotten her Short Take-Off and Landing rating. The damned thing took forever to get airborne.

They stayed low as they flew to their new destination. There was no moon in the sky and no constellations Hunter recognized. How had the ancient navigators felt, he wondered, the first time they crossed from one hemisphere into the other? Without their accustomed stars to guide them, no wonder they thought they were going to fall off the edge of the world.

When they reached the next triangulation point, Hunter set the plane down again. And again, Jack tossed the buoy overboard.

"Got it," Sam said. "One more and I think we'll have her nailed down." He gave Hunter the new coordinates and off they went. This time, the plane was a little easier to get into the air.

Must have been my imagination, Hunter thought as he turned the plane east and headed out over the inky black water.

When the third triangulation point was measured, Hunter left the plane in the water, her engines buzzing while they waited to hear what their destination would be. Stan had to be pretty close, he thought. The Mark V had been moving steadily in this direction since they'd dropped the first buoy. Still, by the time he got here, Hunter and Jack would be long gone. A boat might be fast, but it was no match for a plane. Even an old one like this.

He heard Travis's voice in his ear. He didn't sound happy.

"Gentlemen, I've got some interesting news for you. Over."

Jack's eyes had narrowed. Did he, too, sense something ominous in Travis's tone?

"What is it? Over," Hunter asked.

"We've got a bead on our bogey and Sam's program just spit out his destination." There was a pause. "He's going to Iwo."

"Iwo Jima?" Jack asked. "That's almost six hundred miles away. Over."

"Affirmative. Sam checked the data twice. The same sub has made three runs from Guam to Iwo in the last six months. Best guess tells us that's where he's headed now."

"Travis," Hunter said, "isn't the island a national monument or something? I don't think we can go there without permission."

"Affirmative. I'll call Krauss and have him get us a waiver. But don't forget, our sub's been making runs there with impunity. The island's not inhabited; no one's going to stop us if we just show up."

Jack pressed his transmitter. "If they've gone to Iwo, we'd better get there first and get dug in. The island's full of rat holes. If we wait until they're entrenched, we're fucked. Over."

"Good point. Hold on and let me talk to Stan."

Jack and Hunter waited impatiently while Travis and Stan conversed.

"Hunter? Stan says we can make it there in six hours. At the rate the sub's going, he'll need almost thirty. Leapfrogging won't be a problem for us. What's the range on that bird?"

"About six hundred forty miles—more if the wind's with us—but that won't get us to Iwo."

"What do you want to do?"

Jack held out the map and Hunter checked their position.

"How about if I make a stop on Saipan to refuel?

Shouldn't take more than half an hour and we'll still beat you there. Over."

"Roger that. When you get to Iwo, give yourselves a rest till we get there. We're going to be outnumbered as it is. No sense being tuckered, too."

Jack sat back in his seat, his expression unreadable. Hunter pressed his transmitter.

"Roger that, Travis. Do you have the coordinates?"

"Affirmative. Sam's got them right here."

"Okay," Hunter said. "We'll let you know what we find when we land."

Hunter took down the coordinates and signed off. Then he turned and looked at Jack. "You okay?"

Jack nodded, looking out over the rolling black Pacific. "Iwo Jima. I don't fucking believe it."

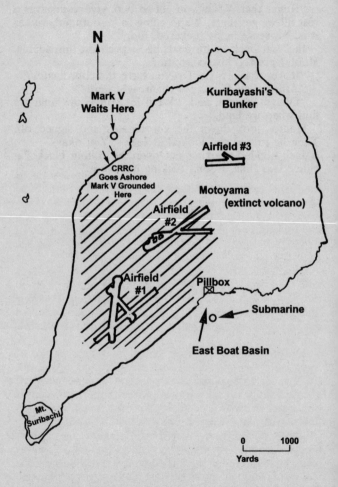

Iwo Jima

N

Mark V
Waits Here

✕ Kuribayashi's
Bunker

Airfield #3

CRRC
Goes Ashore
Mark V Grounded
Here

Airfield
#2

Motoyama
(extinct volcano)

Airfield
#1

Pillbox

Submarine

East Boat Basin

Mt.
Suribachi

0   1000
Yards

⬛ = **Tidorigahara**

Chapter Twenty-five

The crewmen were back in their quarters. Sarah searched the faces of the men as they dragged in from their shifts, stripped off their shirts, and rolled into their bunks. She hadn't seen any of them before. To make room for the girls, the crew must be hot-bunking—the second shift occupying the same beds as the first. Sarah wrinkled her nose as the pungent odor of sweaty bodies filled the room.

Sarah wondered when she would get the chance to talk to Aiyako again. Ever since she'd first spoken to the girls, Sarah had been wondering what Aiyako knew about their abductors' plans. Aiyako hadn't said as much, but it was clear she knew more than she was letting on.

The men were all in their bunks now. One or two of them were snoring, the rest seemed to have passed out from sheer exhaustion. Sarah sat up and maneuvered herself into a sitting position. After dinner, the guards had changed the ropes. Now the girls' hands were tied in front of them. It made moving around a lot easier.

Since arriving here, they'd been taken out of their bunks only once—a supervised trip to the head that was more humiliating for the girls than it was for Sarah. You lost your sense of modesty fast in the Army. Anyone who couldn't eat, sleep, and take a shit with other people watching didn't belong in the military. Sarah had done her best impression of a maiden in distress—enough to give the other girls some cover from prying eyes. In the guise of being a klutz, she'd even managed to knock one of the men into the shower—a prank that the girls had found amusing and that helped to lighten the cheerless mood.

When they returned from the head, they'd been put in different bunks. Sarah was now in the first bunk on the starboard side, crammed in behind a girl named Naoko. Aiyako was in the second bunk, her head at Sarah's feet. Sarah jackknifed and turned her body around in the bunk, taking care not to disturb her bunkmate.

"Aiyako?" she whispered. "Can you hear me?"

Aiyako did not move. "I hear."

"Good," Sarah said, looking around. The men were still sleeping soundly, as were the other girls. "I need to talk to you."

"Okay."

Sarah lifted her head and gazed down at Aiyako. She was the tallest of the girls in the group, and less delicately built than the others. She was also less cowed by their captors. If it came to a fight, she might be a worthwhile ally.

"Remember before, when I asked you if you knew why we were here?"

"I remember."

"It seemed like maybe you knew what the answer was. I just wondered—"

Sarah heard someone in the hallway. Aiyako closed her eyes and tucked her chin down, feigning sleep. Sarah put her own head down and did the same, but kept one eye open to see what was going on.

A man was standing at the door. He wore a tan uniform with an insignia on the collar that Sarah did not recognize. As she watched, he took one step into the room and stopped, looked around, then checked behind him before taking a further step inside.

What's this guy doing? Sarah wondered.

The man was short and round with a fleshy face that had not improved a bad complexion. As he walked, he seemed unsteady on his feet.

Probably drunk.

He sneaked farther into the room. Checking to make sure the men in the bunks were sleeping, he drew closer to the girls. Sarah frowned. Had he come to take them away? No, that didn't make sense. Why send only one man? And why worry about waking the others if he was on official business? The closer he got, the more sure Sarah was that this guy was not supposed to be there. She narrowed her eyes further as he stepped up and stopped next to the head of the opposite bunk.

The little man licked his lips and took a last, furtive look around. Then he slowly reached out and placed a hand on the first girl's breast—it was Gia—groping her gently as she slept.

A pervert!

Sarah wanted to say something, but what? Sam hadn't taught her any phrases she could use to deflect a masher. The man removed his hand from Gia's breast and turned to fondle Naoko.

Honestly, Sarah thought, this had to stop. She was no prude, but this snake-eyed little pig was disgusting. Besides, if he looked closely, he might notice that Sarah had turned herself around in the bed. And if he noticed that, he might suspect that the girls had too much freedom and tie them to their beds. Sarah had to do something. She couldn't let this guy catch her.

She waited until the man's hand had slipped into Naoko's blouse and then she kneed the girl in the back.

"Aiyee!" Naoko opened her eyes and screamed when she saw the groper with his hand down her blouse. The little man jumped, slamming his head into the top bunk and waking the girl above.

"Aiyee!" the other one cried.

The crew came tumbling out of their bunks, bleary-eyed but alert. Three uniformed men came charging into the room.

Angry words were exchanged while the little man tried to explain himself. Gia stood babbling indignantly and Naoko cried. The crewmen muttered among themselves, unhappy at having been awakened. In the confu-

sion, Sarah leaped out of bed and the others followed
suit.

More men came in to see what all the confusion was
about and Sarah quickly counted them. Thirty in here
now—none of them faces she hadn't already seen.

The little man had become belligerent, pointing a finger at Gia, who stamped her foot and protested loudly.
Finally, one of the uniformed men yelled something and
everything went quiet. The confrontation was over. The
rude little man was led away and the crew settled down.

As the guards put the girls back in their bunks Sarah
hung back, trying to get into the same bed as Aiyako.
Seeing what she was up to, Aiyako did the same. It
worked. Sarah and Aiyako were put in the last bunk
together.

It took almost half an hour before things settled down
again. Gia grumbled and spat for a good twenty minutes
before dropping back off to sleep. The rest of them were
too tired to stay awake. As the last of the girls nodded
off, Sarah turned and looked at Aiyako. She didn't know
how much longer they'd have before they got to their
destination, or what might happen once they got there.
She didn't want to let this opportunity pass.

"You were going to tell me why we're here."

Aiyako nodded. "I try." She took a deep breath. "In
Japan, people believe gods rule all things. To make
something happen, you must first give something to
the gods."

"Like a sacrifice, you mean?"

"Yes. Food, wine, many things are pleasing to the di-
vine spirits. If you need only a little, you give a little.
To get much, the gods demand much."

"So, the bigger your wish the bigger your gift has to
be."

Aiyako frowned. "Yes. I think that is what I mean."

"So, are we supposed to give gifts to some god?"

"No," Aiyako said slowly. "We do not give gifts. We
are gifts."

Sarah wrinkled her nose. "We're gifts? To whom?"

"Volcano god." The corners of Aiyako's mouth
turned down. "And I am so sad."

Sarah shook her head. "I don't get it. How can you be a gift to a volcano?"

Then she saw the tears in Aiyako's eyes and she realized what being a gift to a volcano meant.

"You mean *we're* going to be sacrificed to a volcano? As in tossed inside? Burned alive? Kaput?"

The girl's lower lip trembled.

Sarah put her head down and sighed. "Oy! This is worse than I thought."

Chapter Twenty-six

Something was wrong. Hunter calmly went through his mental checklist, trying to figure out what it was. They'd made their stop at Saipan, so fuel wasn't the problem. Hydraulics checked out okay, no warning lights had come on—and yet, like a rider who feels his horse flag under the strain of a long trip, he could feel the Goose's power fading. Over land, the situation might not have alarmed him; but with nothing but water in all directions, it had to be checked out.

He looked at Jack. "I've got to put her down."

"Here?" Jack asked, indicating the ocean.

"Somewhere near here. Check the map and see if you can find us a good spot while I tell Travis."

Jack took out the map and Hunter hailed the boat.

"Boss, this is Hunter. We're having some trouble with the plane. I need to put her down and take a look. Over."

"Copy that. What's your situation?"

"The bird's a little sluggish. Not bad, but I don't want to push my luck."

"Any idea what's wrong with it?"

"I don't know yet. That's why I need to get her on dry land."

"Where are you now?"

"About two hundred and fifty nautical miles north of Saipan. Jack's finding us a place to land."

"Do you want us to vector over and pick you up?"

"Negative. I've got a toolbox and some extra parts. A screwdriver and a roll of duct tape will fix just about anything on one of these old crates. With any luck, I'll get her fixed and still beat you there." He winked at Jack. "Over."

Jack pointed at the map. "We're over the Northern Islands Sanctuary right now. There's a lot of islands, but they're all uninhabited."

Sam's voice cut through the noise. "Hunter, are you sure you want to risk it? Iwo's only another hour away. Over."

The plane faltered. Hunter got her under control, but it was clear she couldn't go much farther.

"I don't think I've got a choice, Sammy. We'll call you when we find a place. Out."

Hunter released his transmitter and looked at Jack.

"Are there any landing strips around here? Even a clear beach would do."

Jack rubbed his forehead, searching the map. "There's nothing but *nothing* around here."

"Keep looking. There's got to be something."

Another minute ticked by. Hunter wrestled with the wheel, trying to keep the plane's nose up as she continued to drift closer to the water. In the beam of the landing lights, the waves seemed to be reaching for them.

"Here's one," Jack said at last. "It's called Asuncion." He pointed to the map. "Right here."

Hunter was still manhandling the control. "What are the coordinates?"

Jack told him.

"Okay, that's about ten miles from here. I think we can do it. Give Travis a call and tell him where we're going. We'll give him a status report once we're down."

"Roger that."

Jack called Travis and told him where they were heading.

"All right," Travis said warily. "But stay in touch. We don't want to lose you two."

"Don't worry about us," Jack said. "We'll be okay. Out."

Chapter Twenty-seven

The sun was a great ball of fire in the east. As it rose, the flames seemed to spread until the entire ocean looked like it was on fire. The light struck Jen's face like a slap.

Red sky at morning, she thought as she held the Mark V on course. She flipped her visor down and kept her eyes on the horizon.

With the addition of Sam's PowerBook, the console was crowded with equipment. The Global Positioning System gave them a continuous readout of their position and Jennifer, as the only other sailor on the team besides Stan, worked the steering toggles to keep them on course. Travis monitored the sonar and the SOSUS data and kept an eye on the map. Normally, driving a Mark V was a three man operation; but these weren't normal conditions.

Sam and Stan were taking their turn sleeping across the two rows of seats in the back of the cabin. The seats were padded, but the gaps between them and the narrow depth made it difficult to get comfortable. Travis and Stan could drop off anywhere, but Jen had not slept well. She rolled her shoulders, trying to work out the kink in her neck.

"How much farther, you suppose?"

Travis checked the map and compared it to the GPS. "Ten minutes, maybe. Maybe less. You okay?"

"Fine."

"Getting hungry? Stan hasn't eaten all the sandwiches yet."

Jennifer shook her head. "Too nervous to eat."

"You sure? Help you keep up your strength."

She smiled. "Okay, *Dad.* Maybe just a bite." She glanced at the computer. "Any word yet from Hunter and Jack?"

Travis pulled a sandwich out of the cooler and shook his head. "Not yet. Knowing them, they're probably on Iwo already, Jack taking a nap and Hunter getting a head start on his tan. When Sam gets up, I'll see if he can hail them."

Off in the distance, Jen spotted something hugging the horizon. A small strip of land with a bump on one end.

"Is that it?" she said, pointing.

"Could be." He lifted his binoculars and took another look. "Yeah, that's definitely Iwo. That's Mount Suribachi on the right."

"It doesn't look like much," Jen said.

"It ain't much. But it's big enough and flat enough to land military aircraft on, and in the middle of an ocean during a war, that's more valuable than gold."

They were closing fast on the island. Travis woke Stan and Sam then returned to his seat.

Jen smiled. "Jack must be having a field day."

"Why's that?"

"Oh, you know how Marines are about Iwo Jima." She indicated the island. "He's probably been reliving the assault since he and Hunter landed."

"I hadn't thought of that." Travis grinned. "You're probably right."

"Is that it?" Stan stepped up beside Jennifer and yawned. "Here, give me the controls."

"Gladly," she said, sliding out of the chair. Jen turned toward Travis. "It's not that big. Shouldn't take long to recon."

"It's big enough."

"Once we get there," Stan said, "I'll need to find a place to leave the boat." He turned around and looked at Sam. "Any way to know which side the sub's going to come up on?"

Sam was sitting on the edge of his seat, looking ill. He shook his head.

"SOSUS doesn't register that close to the islands; but his approach was always from the south-southwest, same as ours. My guess is, he leaves her somewhere on the leeward side."

"Which leaves us the windward," Stan said thoughtfully. "Any word from the plane?"

Travis shook his head. "Nope."

"We've been out of satellite contact for a while," Sam said. He stood on wobbly legs and relieved Travis at the computer. "Even if he tried to contact us, we wouldn't have heard him. Now that we're this close, I can switch from the satellite to a direct communications link." He rubbed his eyes and slumped over the keyboard. "I need caffeine."

Jennifer looked around. "How are we going to anchor this thing?"

"We can't," Stan said. "Someone's going to have to stay on board while we take the landing craft ashore."

Sam lifted his head. "By 'someone' I suppose you mean me?"

"You got it."

He moaned.

"Don't worry," Jen said. "There's some Mountain Dew in the cooler. That ought to keep you happy."

"Dewskis!?" Sam shrieked. "Why didn't you tell me before?"

Jennifer winked at Travis. "We were saving it for an emergency." She walked to the back of the cabin, retrieved a can, and tossed it to Sam.

Ahead off the starboard bow, the island loomed closer. Jennifer picked up Travis's binoculars and examined it. It really was big, she thought. Maybe as much as three miles across. She wondered how much if any of it Jack and Hunter had already reconned. Jack had said the island was full of tunnels; just checking those out could take a whole day.

"You're right, Travis," she said. "We do have a lot of ground to cover. Good thing we got here ahead of our friends."

"Thank God for small favors," Travis agreed. "Any of you see the plane yet?"

"Not me."

"Nope."

Stan goosed the throttle and turned the boat hard to starboard. "I'll make a sweep around the far side. We can look for a place to go ashore and take a look at the airfield, too."

Travis looked at Sam. "Any luck yet hailing Hunter and Jack?"

"Not yet. I just switched over from satellite to direct."

"All right. Give them a call and see what their position is."

The boat swept around to the east, passing through the shadow of Mt. Suribachi. Jennifer shielded her eyes and looked up toward the top of the rocky black cone.

"There's steam coming out of it."

"It's in an active phase right now," Sam said. "I'd been picking up some seismic activity on SOSUS, so I checked the records at the U.S. Geological Survey. In the last year or so, they've had maybe two dozen earthquakes that registered three or more on the Richter scale. During that time, Mount Suribachi has erupted twice."

Jen lifted her eyebrows. "You mean, we're going to have to deal with *lava,* too?"

"No. Suribachi has what are called phreatic eruptions, which means they result from the mixing of magma and sea water. They're pretty dramatic, but no lava's going to come pouring out at you."

"That's a relief."

"Yes. But it's still going to be treacherous. Iwo Jima means 'sulfur island' in Japanese. The interior is pockmarked with steam vents and boiling mud pots. You won't have any lava to deal with, but you're going to have to watch your step."

"Thanks. I'll remember that."

They finished their sweep of the island's windward side and passed over the north end. Travis lowered his BSD and scanned the three old landing strips.

"I don't see them anywhere."

Jen shook her head. "Neither do I."

"Sam?"

"Already working on it."

Jen had a bad feeling as she watched Sam try to contact the plane. What if something had happened to Jack and Hunter? How would they ever find them?

Sam shook his head. "I'm not getting anything."

"Nothing at all?"

"Zip."

"How about if I try," Travis said, reaching behind his ear.

"Don't bother. My transmitter's got twice the range our helmets do. If I can't hail them, you won't be able to, either."

"What are we going to do, then?" Jen asked.

Travis flipped up his visor and frowned. "Let's not worry about it. They've still got a whole day to get here and we've got an island to recon. Sam, switch back to the satellite feed and call them again. In the meantime, Stan, let's find a place to park this tub."

Chapter Twenty-eight

They went ashore on the western side of the island, a strip of land called Tidorigahara, which connects the extinct Motoyama volcano with Mt. Suribachi. Stan drove the Combat Rubber Raiding Craft onto the beach and the three of them jumped out. They pulled it up off the sand, tucked it under a rocky overhang, and covered it with seaweed. Then they strapped on their gear, adjusted their helmets, and prepared to head out.

Travis turned back and looked at the boat. The Mark V was riding high in the water, the gentle bobbing of its pointed bow in jarring juxtaposition to the weapons stations bristling with armament. Sam was at the helm looking sullen and out of place.

"You think he'll be okay?"

Stan snorted. "He'll be fine. The sun's out and the sea's calm. My grandmother could handle it."

"All right. First thing we're going to have to do is establish a base. Jen, you head into the interior and see what the terrain is like, what kind of cover it affords. Keep your eye out for those tunnels Jack talked about. If we can find an intact bunker, it might just serve our purposes. Stan, you scout the area around Suribachi. I have a feeling that volcano's going to seem mighty attractive to our bad guys."

Stan nodded.

"I'm going over to check out the largest air strip, see what kind of shape it's in, and see what kind of cover we can take there. When we were circling the island, I saw some old pillboxes; if Jen doesn't find anything underground, we might be able to use one of those as a base camp. I'd like to find something that's not out in the open.

"Finding water and establishing a latrine are going to be high on our priority list. While you're out there, keep an eye out for any source of fresh water the island might have. In a pinch, we've got desalinization tablets, but they won't go far. Best situation would be to find a spring of some sort." He checked his watch.

"It's oh-seven-twelve now. I'll check in with each of you every hour or so. If you find something or you need help, give me a holler. Once Jack and Hunter get here, we'll buddy up; until then, you're on your own.

"We've got a lot of ground to cover and not much time."

Chapter Twenty-nine

Asuncion Island was a lot like the other islands Jack and Hunter had flown over on their way to Iwo, except that it was older—it took time for a beach to form against a chunk of solid rock. The Goose sat on the long narrow strip of gray, its wheels sunk deep into the soft sand while Hunter crouched on the wing, hovering over the starboard nacelle. He had the engine cowl open, trying to find out why the plane had lost power last night. Jack was stretched out along the wing, holding the spotlight, trying not to think about Travis and the others up on Iwo Jima.

Jack looked around. The beach ran the length of Asuncion's leeward side and from there rose steeply toward the inland to the top of an almost perfect volcanic cone. Jack had reconned the island that morning and found a few small trees and some windswept shrubs farther inland; but not much more. They had fish to eat and plenty of birds they could catch if they needed to; but without water, they'd be hurting soon. They had to get the plane fixed—fast.

"Move the light up a little."

Jack pointed the beam onto the place where Hunter had moved his hands.

Landing had been the worst. Going down over the ocean, Jack was sure they'd never make it to the island, and the excitement had taken its toll. Once on shore, he and Hunter had had only enough strength to crawl into the back and fall asleep. They hadn't even tried to radio Travis and the others. Now, they needed the generator to power the spotlight so they couldn't contact them at all. In the cold light of day, the problem with the plane seemed bigger than either of them had imagined.

"How much longer you think this is going to take?"

"Not long." Hunter glanced at him. "Why? Aren't you enjoying this?"

"Are you?"

"Of course."

Jack gave him a disbelieving stare.

"Look," Hunter said, rolling onto his side, "planes these days are so slick you practically need a Ph.D. to fix one. But with this baby"—he patted the Goose—"all a man needs is his wits and a couple of tools."

"You really get off on that, huh?"

"Damn straight." Hunter rolled back and reached his arm into the nacelle. "When I was a kid, I had an old sixty-eight Camaro that I used to carry my surfboards in. Every free minute I wasn't on a wave, I was working on my car. Man, that thing was cherry."

Jack shrugged. As a kid, his only experience with cars had been hotwiring them for joyrides. Furthermore, he thought any teenage boy who voluntarily spent his free time working on cars was about a quart shy of testosterone.

"Glad to see you're enjoying yourself."

Jack was restless, trying to keep the light on Hunter's hands as he poked and prodded and tested. Adding to his discomfort was the fact that the island's inhabitants apparently found them irresistible. Pelicans and cormorants, sitting on their nests in the surrounding rocks, squawked like old women gossiping on their doorsteps while they watched the two men and their odd-looking contraption. Overhead, seagulls screeched and wheeled, landing occasionally to strut along the fuselage and examine the plane. Jack tried to shoo them away, but the birds had no fear of humans.

"Hold still, Jack. I can't see."

Jack grumbled and adjusted the beam. He didn't want to hold still; he wanted to get to Iwo. That's where a

Marine belonged—not stranded here with a bunch of goddamned pelicans. Once it was fixed, Hunter said the plane could make it to Iwo Jima in an hour or less. Jack hoped he was right. He didn't want to miss the fun.

Hunter leaned back and searched his tools for a screwdriver.

"What's the matter?"

Jack surveyed the beach. "I'm thinking of having a seagull sandwich for lunch."

Hunter laughed. "I don't think I'm that hungry yet." He found the screwdriver and gave Jack an appraising look. "What's bugging you?"

Jack shrugged. "Just thinking."

"About what?"

"The war."

"What war?"

"*The* war. In the Pacific. Iwo Jima, remember?"

Hunter nodded. "Ah."

"Ever since Sam said the sub was heading to Iwo, I've had this strange feeling. You know, to a Marine, Iwo's not just another battlefield. It's like holy ground or something. Guess a flyboy like you wouldn't understand."

"Sure, I understand. I don't know the details of the battle, but I know it was bloody."

"Want me to tell you about it?"

"Will it make you hold still?"

Jack grinned. "Guaranteed."

"All right then," Hunter said, reaching into the nacelle and tugging on a wire. "But I've got to warn you, I know how the story ends."

Jack nodded and moved the spotlight to where Hunter was checking the fuel lines. He took a deep breath.

"It was the largest invasion of the Pacific—a hundred and ten thousand Marines in eight hundred and eighty ships sailed to Iwo from Hawaii in forty days. . . ."

Chapter Thirty

Stan headed uphill, making his way over the rocky crags
that made up the southern tip of the island. Dark gray,
pockmarked boulders were the only thing underfoot.
The whole place smelled faintly like rotten eggs; but
every so often, Stan would pass a vent hole and the
stench would become unbearable. Tufts of gray lichen
grew on the rocks, turning yellow around the mouths of
the gas vents. The ground was hot. Off to his left, he
could hear the low rumbling of the volcano.

Stan had never been this close to a live volcano before. As he climbed the cinder cone, he wondered what
it would look like inside. Would it be like a witch's cauldron, bubbling with some sulfurous brew? Or full of fire,
red and raging?

As he neared the top, Stan started circling around
toward the northern end of Mt. Suribachi. The ground
was treacherous. Ashes and small stones shifted under
his feet with every step. He crested the rise and looked
out toward the northwest, across the southernmost airfield, and over the ocean. From here, there was nothing
but water until you got to Japan. No wonder Iwo had
been such an important piece of real estate, he thought.
Without an airfield in the South Pacific, the allies didn't
have a hope of striking Tokyo. With it, everything was
possible.

There was a plaque embedded in the ground, marking
the place where the Marines had raised the American

flag after the battle of Iwo Jima. Stan bent down and brushed crumbs of volcanic ash from the bold lettering. Twenty thousand men had lost their lives in that battle— one of the bloodiest of the Second World War. He took his helmet off and went down on one knee, said a brief prayer, then crossed himself.

Something shiny caught his eye.

It was a ring. A small, gold circle with a single pearl set in it. A girl's ring. He reached forward and picked it up, turning it over as the light made rainbows on the pearl's surface.

There was only one reason a little girl's ring would be up here, he thought. He put his helmet back on and pressed his transmitter.

"Travis, it's Stan. I think I've got something. Over."

"What is it, Stan?"

"A ring," he said examining the bauble in his hand. He wondered what had happened to its owner. "I found it near the memorial marker at the top of Mount Suriba-chi. I'm wondering if it might have belonged to one of the kidnapped girls."

"Could be. But why up there?"

"Good question." Stan looked down the path that led away from the top of the mountain. "There's a trail that leads up here from the invasion beach. I suppose a tour-ist might have left it. Doesn't seem likely, though."

He stood up and looked around. This area seemed more recently trod than the rest of the island. Maybe the kidnappers had brought the girls up here. But why?

"How about if I look around and see if I can find anything else?"

"Good idea. Call me if you do. Travis out."

Stan opened his breast pocket and slipped the ring inside.

0827 hours,
Invasion Beach, Iwo Jima

Travis signed off and returned to exploring the pillbox he'd found near the runway. The emplacement was at the north end of the eastern beach—the one everyone called Invasion Beach since the war—and there was an identical one on the south end. The Japanese had positioned themselves here when the American troops came ashore, picking them off with machine gun fire as they came storming off their landing craft. Seeing the broad expanse of black sand, the almost unimpeded view, it was no wonder that so many men had died here, Travis thought. The wonder was that any of them had lived.

The pillboxes were in ruins, and they weren't big enough to set up a base camp in. They might be fascinating, but they wouldn't get the group any closer to its objective. Travis stepped reluctantly away from the corrupted steel-reinforced concrete and continued his recon of airfield #1.

The airstrip seemed to be in good condition. Travis bent down and picked up a stone. The tarmac was littered with small rocks and other debris that would have made it difficult if not impossible for the Lear to set down. Probably best that Hunter had gotten that amphib.

But where was the amphib? They'd heard nothing from either Hunter or Jack since last night. Were they still on Asuncion, fixing the plane, or feeding the sharks somewhere out in the ocean?

Damn! Travis wished he'd been able to requisition a chopper from Anderson Air Force Base. No. What he really wished was that this whole mission didn't have to be so much of a secret in the first place. Even getting the sonobuoy had been conducted as a sleight of hand, telling the XO at Marianas that they needed the buoy to help conduct undersea research for the local university. Having to keep his cards close to his vest had made Travis hesitant to do what he thought was right and eager to find a quick solution when he should have been more deliberate. Worse yet, he knew that whatever he did, it was going to be second-guessed by someone in the State Department if everything didn't come out just the way they wanted it to.

As much as he hated to sound like Stan, this mission really was starting to feel like a goatfuck.

But Travis had a tough hide. If some candy-assed bureaucrat wanted to play Monday-morning quarterback from behind his desk in Washington, that was fine. He could take the hit. What he couldn't take was the thought of losing one of his people. It was bad enough having Sarah gone, but not knowing where Jack and Hunter were was killing him. The TALON members had become like family to Travis. And since Lavonne and the kids moved out, he didn't have much family left.

He'd come to the end of the runway. The ruins of a stone tower were still standing, and around that more fortifications. The ground was littered with debris. Travis found dented shell casings, rusty C-ration cans, the hilt of a broken knife, even a belt buckle with bits of rotted webbing still threaded through it. He bent down and sifted a handful of sand through his fingers. It was as if time had stopped and the ghosts of this place were still here, ready to pick up the things they'd left behind and begin the battle all over again. He squinted up at the sun. Maybe Hunter and Jack had checked in with Sam. He pressed his transmitter.

"Sam? Travis here. Any word yet from the plane? Over."

"Nothing. I've sent a message every half hour since you left. Still no reply."

Travis nodded and slapped his hand on his pants. The breeze picked up, riffling his shirt and blowing sand in his eyes. The sub wouldn't get to Iwo for at least another eighteen hours. Maybe he should send Stan back to Asuncion to see if he could find them.

And if he couldn't, then what? Then Travis and Jen would have to take care of the bogeys all by themselves. No. He couldn't risk it. He was already shorthanded as it was. If Hunter and Jack showed up, great. If they didn't, he'd just have to make do. He wasn't going to risk losing another man.

Travis took a deep breath and pressed his transmitter. "Uh, Roger that, Sam. Keep trying to hail them. In the meantime, we'll keep looking for a bivouac. Out."

Chapter Thirty-one

Jen had found the first tunnel only half an hour after leaving the beach. Partially collapsed, it was useless from the team's point of view; but it had given her hope that there might be others, and that one of them might lead to a bunker they could use as a base.

She'd been able to follow the second tunnel for over five hundred yards before coming to a dead end. Littered with bits of metal, parts of weapons, and even a few broken bones, it was an eerie, cramped hideaway that she'd needed her thermal viewer to properly reconnoiter. Coming up out of the ground after walking through that one had been a relief.

Now she was on her third try, and this time the tunnel looked like something they could use. It was high enough in the middle that she could almost stand up straight, and wide enough that two people could pass without brushing against one another. The walls were solid rock—no sand inside at all—and as impregnable as steel. A bomb could go off overhead and she wouldn't know it. Whoever built this tunnel knew what he was doing.

Using her compass, Jennifer was able to guess where she was relative to the surface. Although the tunnel had its fair share of twists and turns, she'd been traveling in a generally northward direction for what had been, by her estimation, more than a mile. Right now, she should be somewhere under the airfield.

She stepped carefully around another pile of debris—a mess kit and a rifle barrel. Had the Japanese spent the entire battle down here? she wondered. The island was considered a war memorial now, so no one could disturb what remained of the battle, but why hadn't anyone come through before and cleared this place out?

Jen stopped and flipped up her visor, wiping her brow with her sleeve. There were cobwebs clinging to her uniform and her back was killing her; but she couldn't go back until she'd found the end of the tunnel. They needed to get a base camp set up and make plans; time was running out.

Up ahead, Jen saw a shaft of light stabbing out of the darkness, falling onto the floor of the tunnel. Was that the way out? She hurried forward, her heart pounding with excitement.

The light was coming from one of the smaller feeder tunnels that Jennifer had seen since starting down. It jogged off to the left and rose steeply to the surface. Jen made a mental note of its position. If she did find a bunker at the end of the main passageway, it would be good to know all the other routes to the surface besides the way she'd just come.

The rock here was black. Jennifer rubbed her fingers over it and they came away greasy and sooty. She sniffed, noting the faint petroleum smell that still clung to the walls. When the Japanese had not come out of their hiding places, the American troops had turned their flame throwers on the tunnels to rout their enemy. You didn't need more evidence than this to convince yourself that war was hell. She brushed her hand on her pants and continued her recon.

From here, the tunnel sloped downward. Jennifer stepped carefully as the path curved to the right and the shaft of light was left behind. Surely, this was leading to something, but what? She reached up and pressed the transmitter behind her ear.

"Travis, this is Jen. Can you hear me? Over."

"Loud and clear, Jen. Something wrong? Over."

"I'm in a tunnel and I wanted to see if being underground affected my signal."

"Not on my end. Where are you?"

Jen glanced at her compass. Too bad the GPS wouldn't work underground. She'd just have to ballpark a guess.

"I should be about five hundred yards from the northern tip of runway number three."

"That's pretty close. Mind if I join you?"

"Not at all. I just passed an opening a few yards back. Give me a second and I'll poke my head out. Out."

Jen turned around and headed back the way she'd come. The slope was steeper than she'd realized on her way down. Good thing the walls were solid. She'd hate to think what would happen if there was a cave-in.

The feeder tunnel was on her right. She lifted her visor and stepped into the shaft of light, shielding her eyes against the glare.

At the end of the tunnel, she was still ten feet below the surface. To get out, she'd have to go straight up. Jennifer searched the wall for a toehold, found it, then stepped up and pulled herself toward the light. The walls were looser here; she turned her face away as bits of rock and lichen rained down on her.

Only a couple of feet to go. Jennifer looked up, trying to find another handhold. The sun was in her eyes; she had to reach up blindly and grope around until she found one. There. It was a nice rock—good and smooth—with dents where she could get her fingers inside. She moved her toe up the wall and pulled herself up.

Suddenly, the rock in her hand gave way. Jennifer lost her footing and tumbled back down into the tunnel. The nice smooth rock that had seemed like such a good handhold tumbled down after her and fell into her lap. She looked at it and let out an involuntary scream.

"Jen? Jennifer, where are you?" Travis's voice sounded close.

Jen took a deep breath and swallowed.

"I'm okay," she said sheepishly. "Just took a tumble, that's all." She stood and picked up the "rock" that had fallen into her lap. It was an intact human skull. The forehead was blackened, the rest was chalky white. No holes or breaks in the cranium. This guy must have faced the flames.

A shadow crossed overhead. Jennifer looked up and saw Travis peering down at her.

"You all right?" he asked.

"Sure." Jen shoved the skull up at him. "I'm just doing my road show version of Hamlet. Want to join me?"

Travis jumped into the hole.

"Nice souvenir," he said, examining the skull. "But I was looking for something the kids would enjoy."

Jen set the skull down and pointed back the way she'd come.

"There's a bigger tunnel down there that I've been following for almost an hour. I think it might lead to a bunker."

"Let's have a look. Stan's checking on the boat and I haven't found a thing we can use for a base camp. This is the best lead we've had so far."

They were in luck. The tunnel bottomed out only a hundred yards farther down.

"It looks like a door," Jennifer said.

Travis tried the bolt. "These hinges are pretty rusty; I think I can pry it open. Give me some room."

Jennifer stepped back and watched as Travis tugged on the door. "This place is a long way underground."

Travis grunted. "Yeah. Nothing but solid rock between us and the surface." He slid his fingers between the wood and the rock and gave the door another tug. It came open with a nerve-jangling screech.

"My God, what is it?" Jen said, peering over Travis's shoulder.

Travis pulled out a flashlight and they stepped inside.

"Well, I can't be sure; but right off hand, I'd say it's Kuribayashi's command center."

Chapter Thirty-two

"The Air Force had been pounding the hell out of Iwo for a week trying to soften her up," Jack said. "The island's nothing but a great big volcanic rock—you'd think it would have been pulverized—but Kuribayashi was a fucking genius. He and his men were barely touched by the bombing."

Jack's instincts had been right—talking about the battle had made him feel better—and Hunter was happy because his light didn't move around so much. In the last couple of hours, he'd cleared a clogged fuel line and replaced a spark plug. How much longer, Jack wondered, before they could start her up again?

"Why not?"

"Why not what?"

"Why weren't they touched by the bombing?"

"They were all underground. Twenty-one thousand of them. They'd dug fifteen hundred rooms and sixteen miles of tunnels into that island. Kuribayashi's command center was under seventy-five feet of solid rock. Sun Tzu says, 'The experts in defense conceal themselves as under the nine-fold earth.' Well, that's just what they did. The Japs dug in under the earth and just waited for the American troops to come ashore." Jack shook his head. "While we were dropping all those bombs, old Kuribayashi must have been laughing at us."

"Hand me the Crescent wrench, will you?"

Jack set the light down, jumped off the wing, and pulled the wrench out of the toolbox. He handed it up to Hunter. The wind picked up and blew some sand from his sleeve into the nacelle.

"Careful! I don't need any more problems in here."

"Sorry." Jack pulled his arm back and slapped the sand off of it.

Hunter said he still felt confident that this delay wouldn't keep them from getting to Iwo ahead of the sub, and Jack hoped he was right. Making the trip to Iwo Jima would be like going on a pilgrimage. He climbed back onto the wing and resumed his post.

"So what was the deal with Kuribayashi? How did he expect to get his men off the island?"

Jack shook his head. "He didn't. Every man was told that the point of his being there was to kill ten Americans before he died."

"That's it?"

"That's it. Before they left for Iwo Jima, they all said good-bye to their families—even Kuribayashi."

"What the hell kind of strategy is that?"

"A brilliant one. No one fights harder than the man who's fighting to stay alive—even if it's for only another minute."

Hunter turned his head and wiped his hands on a rag. "Sun Tzu again, right?"

"Right. A soldier always has hope, right up to the second he buys it. What Kuribayashi did was put his men in the mindset of the doomed. He knew they'd fight hardest that way. If those soldiers thought they had any hope of escape, they'd have been holding something in reserve. By freeing them of the obligation to keep themselves alive, he got all the fight out of them that he could."

Hunter frowned. "Kind of makes you wonder, though. If Kuribayashi knew he was going to lose anyway, why did he bother? Why not make a stand somewhere where he could win?"

"I don't think he was sure he'd lose. Like I said, hope dies hard. If his plan had worked, he'd have wiped out every American soldier who stepped onto the beach at Iwo. But what he really wanted was to make the conflict so bloody that the American people would demand that the war be ended. And it was bloody. The Marines' finest hour." Jack sighed. "You know, sometimes I think I was born too late."

"Me too." Hunter closed the engine cowl.

"Is it fixed?"

"Should be."

They jumped off the wing and Hunter scraped away the sand that had accumulated around the wheels. He opened the cockpit door.

"Come on, let's give her a try."

Jack ran around and got into the co-pilot's seat. He put on his seatbelt; Hunter did the same. Then Jack covered his ears as the engine turned over and the amphib roared to life. Hunter checked the gauges, nodded at Jack, and gave him a thumbs-up. He reached down and pushed the throttle forward. The Goose lurched ahead and began tottering along the shore.

"All right!" Jack yelled, punching the air. "We are in business!"

They taxied down the beach, picking up speed, scattering birds and crabs in their wake. Hunter grinned, checking the flaps and the dials and all the other stuff that Jack didn't understand or care to. All he could think about was getting to Iwo. Iwo! In an hour, he'd be walking on sacred ground. It was almost too good to be true.

Hunter turned the plane around and taxied back the way they'd come. Then he turned off the engine and undid his safety belt.

"Looks like everything's checked out," he said. "Only thing left is to take her up."

"Great! Let's do it."

"We can't." Hunter looked out over the water and pointed. "Not until that thing gets past us."

Jack turned and looked out over the ocean. A bank of clouds had moved in, darkening the western sky. When had that happened?

"What the fuck?"

"Don't worry. It's probably just a squall. Once it hits, we should be out of it in an hour. In the meantime," Hunter said, "let's see if we can find something to tie the plane down with."

"I thought you said it was no big deal," Jack said.

Hunter grinned. "I didn't say that. I said it wouldn't last long."

Chapter Thirty-three

The old priest's mood was grim. He'd been reading the signs all morning and every time they said the same thing: the gods did not favor this trip. It left him no choice. He must go and tell the shogun.

The shogun was in the captain's cabin, a cramped space with few amenities and even fewer personal items. The priest noticed with pleasure, though, that the gods had not been forgotten. A shrine sat on top of the small writing desk and flower petals were strewn around the picture of Amaterasu in her glory.

The priest bowed deeply from the waist and waited to be acknowledged.

"Come in, come in," the shogun said heartily. "I was just paying homage to the goddess in hopes she would bless our sacred journey."

The old man's eyes darted around the room. He had seen men lose their heads when the shogun flew into a rage; the hearty welcome was no reassurance.

"Actually, it is a sign from the goddess that brings me here."

The shogun frowned. "Go on."

The old man swallowed. "I have checked the signs three times and every time they come out the same."

"The same *what*? Speak, man!"

"Our journey is in peril. Amaterasu is displeased."

"Displeased? How can she be displeased? Have I not given tribute to her temple lords and food to the monks who tend her holy places? For what reason would she move against me? Tell me now, or lose your head."

The priest bowed. "The signs are unclear, noble one, but I believe it is because Amaterasu is angry that you have given so many of her virgins to Suribachi-yama. I fear . . . I fear she may curse our endeavors if she is not placated."

The shogun's eyes were wild. He was so close to achieving the power he craved. To have it snatched away at this late date would dishonor him and his family for generations.

"Tell me what I must do to be in the goddess's favor once again."

The priest licked his lips. "I believe a special sacrifice is in order. One for Amaterasu only. A virgin of her own as offering."

"Yes. That's good." The shogun nodded, rubbing his chin. "Suribachi-yama's belly is getting full; one less virgin will not leave him wanting. Guard!"

The shogun's bodyguard appeared at the door and bowed low.

"Bring one of the maidens to me. Let no one see you. Hurry!"

The man bowed again and hurried down the gangway.

The shogun smiled at the holy man. "My thanks for warning me of this impending disaster. Go. Read the signs again in an hour. I think you'll see the goddess has changed her mind."

The priest bowed and backed out the door.

The shogun watched him go, feeling his resolve harden like steel. The gods must be with him in this enterprise. They must! He had come so far. Nothing must be allowed to stand in his way.

The sound of footsteps roused him. He turned and saw his bodyguard hurrying toward him, pulling a tiny, cowed girl behind him. The man bowed at the door, forcing the girl to do the same.

"Master, it is as you have ordered."

The shogun gave a curt nod. "You may go."

The man turned and disappeared, leaving the girl

standing wide-eyed at the entrance to the shogun's
quarters.

"My dear," the man purred. "You are shivering. Do
not be afraid. Here, come inside. Sit down."

The girl nodded gently and sat on the bunk, giving it
a tentative bounce.

The shogun turned his back and opened the drawer of
his desk. Reaching in, he removed his *naginata,* favored
weapon of the *daimyo* for assassinating enemies and
eliminating rivals.

"You are being well cared for, I presume?"

The blade glinted under the small reading lamp. The
shogun picked it up and slid the point up his sleeve.

The girl rubbed the places on her wrists where they
had been recently bound. "Yes."

"Good," the man said, turning back. The knife in his
hand was cold and razor sharp. "But of course, it's not
the same as home. With your mother and father."

The girl's lower lip began to quiver and tears filled
her eyes.

"There there," he said. "Don't cry."

The shogun pulled her to her feet and slid his left arm
behind her back.

So young, he thought. *So young and innocent.*

"Everything will be over soon. Then you can go home.
Would you like that?"

The girl looked up and nodded.

The blade was out. The shogun thrust. The girl's smile
became a grimace as the knife slipped under her breast
bone and into her heart. The shogun felt that heart beat
once, then twice more before she collapsed in his arms.

Turning to the shrine, he bowed and laid the girl's
body in front of it.

"Amaterasu, I give you your sacrifice."

Chapter Thirty-four

"Boss, can you hear me? This is Sam. Over."

Travis, Stan, and Jen were just finishing their underground base camp. Kuribayashi's bunker was perfect. Not only was it under a thick layer of rock reinforced with concrete, but there was plenty of room to stow their gear. There was no fresh water on the island, but Jennifer had desalinated sea water in their canteens and Travis and Stan had dug a latrine outside. For the first time since they got there, Travis felt secure. He reached up and pressed his transmitter.

"Travis here. What is it, Sam? Over."

"I think we've got a problem."

Travis frowned. "Be more specific. Over."

"There's a storm coming in. I checked the NOAA database and it looks like we're right in its path."

Stan looked at Travis. "Let me talk to him."

"Go for it."

"Sam, Powczuk here. How's the boat doing?"

"Okay so far, but the water's getting choppy. I don't think I can handle it in a storm. Over."

"Try and keep it in place," Stan said. "I'll be there in ten minutes."

"Roger that. I'll be waiting. Out."

Stan looked at Travis. "I'd better get out there before the little weenie runs her into the rocks."

"What are you going to do?"

"Get Sam to shore and then take her out until the storm blows over."

"And then what?"

"Then I'll come back here. What's the problem?"

"The problem is, we don't know how long this storm is going to last; but we do know when that sub's coming up. I can't afford to be one man short when the shit goes down."

"Hunter and Jack will be here by then."

"Maybe. Or maybe they'll have to wait for the storm to pass them, too. I'm sorry, Stan. I can't let you ride it out on the water. I need you here."

Stan's lips were tight. "So what do you expect me to do?"

"Beach her."

"What? That could ruin her!"

"And having you out there when the sub arrives could ruin the mission. You heard me. The only choices are to beach the Mark Five or cut her loose. If we cut her loose, we lose her for sure. If she's beached, at least she'll still be salvageable."

Stan's face was suffused with red. "Is that an order, sir?"

Travis sighed. "Stan, don't."

"Is that an order? *Sir.*"

"Yes. That's an order."

Stan gritted his teeth. "I'll go get Sam and bring the Mark Five ashore." He gave Travis a smart salute and turned on his heel.

Jen's mouth fell open as she watched Stan leave.

Travis shook his head. "Don't worry about it. He's just mad because he thinks he'll look bad to his SEAL buddies. No matter what we tell them, they'll say he ran it up onto the beach by accident. He'll be the butt of some jokes for a while; but he'll live. In the meantime, we're going to have to make some room for Sam."

1049 hours,
northwest coast of Iwo Jima

Stan headed for the boat, angry and sullen. Beach the boat? What the hell was Travis thinking? The Mark V was a precision machine—one of only a handful in the world—beaching it would be like desecrating a holy relic. There had to be a better way. He just hadn't figured out what it was yet.

Sam waved at him as he crested the rise. The wind was blowing harder now than it had been and the boat was being tossed like a tub toy on the choppy water. Stan waved back and started tearing the seaweed off the CRRC. There was a flash in the distance and a rumble of lightning, and the first few drops of rain splattered on the rocks.

Stan pushed the CRRC into the water and started the engine. The sky was getting dark fast. He glanced back over his shoulder and was surprised to see streaks of lightning crisscrossing the oncoming clouds. Just how fast was the front moving, anyway? He opened the throttle and steered the inflatable toward the Mark V.

Sam was frantic.

"I can't get my PowerBook off the console!" he yelled as the CRRC pulled up alongside the boat. "You gorillas overtightened the screws."

"How's the boat doing?"

"Did you hear what I said? I can't get the computer off the fucking console! My equipment's going to be ruined!"

Stan steadied the CRRC as it rose and fell on the waves. "Cool your jets; I'll get it off in a second. Help me put this baby aboard first."

Sam steadied the Mark V while Stan brought the rubber craft astern and drove the CRRC up into its berth on the back of the boat. Stan secured the landing craft and walked over to the console.

"Where's the wrench?"

Sam handed it to him. "Where's Travis?"

"Back at base camp." Stan examined the computer. Sam had already shut the system down and disconnected the satellite dish. All that was left was the grunt work.

"Who's going to watch the boat?" Sam asked.

Stan crawled under the console and flipped himself over, then reached up underneath the dash, feeling around for the bolts.

"I'll have this off in a second," he said. "Get the rest of your gear together and put it in the CRRC."

"Stan," Sam repeated. "Who's going to watch the boat?"

Stan took a deep breath. "Nobody."

"Nobody?"

"You heard me."

Stan slid the wrench over the nut and twisted. Sam was right, it had been overtightened. He hoped it wasn't stripped.

"We can't leave the boat out here during the storm. It'll be smashed to pieces."

"We're not going to leave it out here," Stan said, trying the bolt again. "We're going to beach it."

Stan readjusted the wrench and turned, a short burst of power that seemed to loosen the bolt ever so slightly.

"Beach it? Whose brilliant idea was that?"

Stan smirked. "Not mine."

The first bolt was off. Stan quickly removed the others and sealed them in his front pocket. Then he unhooked the PowerBook and handed it to Sam, who set it in its shockproof case and tied it into the CRRC. The rain was coming down harder now and the boat was lurching like a drunk on a trampoline.

Stan took the conn. "Strap yourself in. It's going to be a rough ride."

Sam double-checked the equipment and staggered forward, sliding into the navigator's chair and putting on his safety belt.

Stan checked the Global Positioning System. The Mark V had drifted closer to the shore since he'd gotten there. He opened the throttle and turned the boat around, trying to give himself some room to maneuver.

The squall was right on top of them now. Stan could barely see the island through the sheets of rain that surrounded them on all sides. It was like looking through a shower curtain—he could make out the shape of the island, but not its features. In fact, he couldn't even tell where the black sandy beach ended and the rocks began. He heard something in his ear.

"Stan? This is Travis. It sounds like a train's passing overhead. Where are you? Over."

Stan pressed his transmitter, holding the wheel steady with his free hand.

"I'm still trying to get the boat ashore. I'll let you know when we're there. Out."

"Stan? You're breaking up. Is the boat ashore yet? Over."

Stan looked at Sam. "Will you try and get through to him? If I take my hand off this wheel again, I'm going to fucking lose her."

Sam pressed his finger behind his ear. "Travis, this is Sam. The storm's wreaking havoc with our transmitters. Don't worry about the boat. We're taking her in right now. We'll call you when we're on shore. Over."

"Damn it, Stan, stop screwing around! Beach that goddamned boat and get back here on the double. That's an order!"

Sam looked at Stan. "You want to talk to him?"

"No. Just tell him we're almost there."

Sam nodded and pressed his transmitter. "Roger that, Travis. We'll be there ASAP. Out."

Stan had the boat in position now, the bow pointed straight toward the island, perpendicular to the beach. With any luck, the Mark V would hit a patch of soft sand and stop before much damage was done. As soon as the storm passed, Stan could put her back into the water. She'd be scratched, maybe even dented; a little sand rash never killed a Mark V.

He looked at Sam. "Hang on tight! This is going to be a rough one!"

The boat surged forward, pounding the waves as it drove for the beach. The water was black and the sun was gone. As the rain pelted the windshield, Stan squinted at the island, trying to make out its features. It was like looking at a mirage. The harder he tried to make it out, the less sure he was that the damned thing was even out there.

They hit another wave. The bow slapped the water, rose up, and went down hard.

"My equipment's starting to move!" Sam shrieked.

"Don't worry about it! It'll be okay!"

"But it might go overboard!"

"If it does, there's nothing we can do about it. Leave it alone!"

Sam was turned around in his chair, watching the equipment anxiously.

"Turn around and hold on!"

Stan gripped the wheel. Another wave rolled underneath them, lifting the boat high into the air. The Mark V rode the crest for a moment, paused at the top, and crashed down again. Stan wished he knew the topography of the surrounding area better. How deep was the water under them now? Did the island rise gradually from the ocean floor, or thrust up abruptly? The way the waves were swelling this close to shore, his guess was the latter. Right now, in fact, he was counting on it.

The rain cleared for an instant, and for the first time Stan could see the shore clearly. Only a couple hundred yards to go.

"Hold on, Sam! We're almost there!"

Then a huge wave slapped them broadside. Stan struggled to keep the boat from swamping. Beside him, Sam was screaming about his equipment.

"I've got to get the dish! It's going to fall overboard!"

"Forget about the goddamned dish!"

"We can't afford to lose it!"

Stan stared at the beach. Impact was only seconds away. "There isn't time! Leave it alone!"

"I can't! I've got to get it!"

Sam took off his seatbelt.

"Sam, no!"

Suddenly, the beach rose up like a monstrous black curtain in front of them. The impact threw Stan forward onto the wheel. He felt his arms collapse under him as he pitched forward. The wheel hit him in the diaphragm, knocking the wind out of him. The Mark V plowed up onto the shore and stopped.

Rain ran down the sides of Stan's face and into his mouth as he struggled for air. His gut hurt and his arms were shaking, but he'd made it. And from the looks of things, so had the Mark V. He reached down and turned the engine off.

"There," he said, lifting his head. "That wasn't so bad, was it, Sam?" He turned. "Sam?"

The navigator's seat was empty.

"Shit!" Stan jumped up and ran to the back of the boat. "Sam! Where are you?"

The rain was still coming down hard. Stan cupped his hands around his mouth and yelled.

"Sam!" Then he remembered his transmitter. He reached up and pressed it. "Sam? Where are you, buddy? I can't see you."

No answer. He tried again.

"Sam? This is Stan. Where the hell are you?"

"Stan? This is Travis. What's going on? Over."

"Nothing. Don't worry about it. I just lost Sam."

"What do you mean *you lost him*?"

"I lost him, goddamn it! Okay? You asked me to beach the goddamned boat and I did. Sam just fell overboard. Give me a fucking second and I'll find him! Out."

Stan jumped out of the boat and searched the shoreline. Why wasn't Sam answering him? Was it his transmitter, or was he out cold? He remembered Sam telling Jen that Sarah's signal couldn't go through water. Was Sam underwater? Jesus, if anything happened to that little geek, Stan would be filling out paperwork from now until judgment day.

He heard something behind him.

"Stan! Over here!"

Stan turned in the direction he'd heard Sam's voice, but in the relentless downpour, he couldn't see more than a few feet in front of him.

"Sam? Where are you?"

"Over here. Near the rocks."

Stan started to run.

"I still can't see you! Say something!"

"I'm over here!"

Stan took another step and pulled up short. Sam was lying in a heap only a few feet away. Another step and Stan would have been right on top of him.

He stepped forward and bent down. Sam was sitting up, his face and chest covered with sticky black sand.

"You okay?"

"I'm not sure. My ankle hurts."

"Let me take a look at it."

Stan tugged Sam's pantleg up and looked at the quickly swelling ankle.

"Is it broken?"

"I can't tell. Let's get you to base camp and take a look at it there."

The gear was still in the CRRC. Stan shoved it into a rucksack and tied it onto Sam's back as the rain beat down on them.

"What are you doing? I can't carry all that shit. I don't even know if I can walk!"

"That's okay," Stan said, grinning. "You're with a SEAL, remember?" He bent down and hoisted Sam onto his shoulders. "Walking is optional."

Chapter Thirty-five

Sarah stared at the bulkhead, its gunmetal gray paint blistered and peeling, and wondered what had happened to Tomomi. A guard had taken the girl away half an hour ago and there'd been no sign of her since. Sarah felt a special fondness for Tomomi. At eleven, she was the youngest of the kidnapped girls. She hoped they'd hear something from her soon. When the shit hit the fan, it would be harder to get the girls to safety if they weren't all together.

They'd been underway now for more than a day and the wait was killing Sarah. Dinner—a thick fish soup served over rice—had been over hours ago; by her reckoning, it was now sometime in the early morning. The rest of the girls were sound asleep; but Sarah hadn't been able to rest since Aiyako's revelation.

The crew's bunks were empty now—every man was at his station. Once in a while a man would walk down the gangway outside their door and glance in at the prisoners; but for the most part they were left alone. In the twenty-four hours she'd been held captive, Sarah had kept count of every man she'd seen; as near as she could tell, there were forty-five men on board. Too many for her to take by herself; but not too many for the team.

If they were still with her.

Sarah sighed and rolled over onto her other side. After the girls' last trip to the head, the guards had tied their hands behind their backs again. She couldn't lie on her back and if she tried to lie on her stomach, she couldn't breathe. As Sarah adjusted her position on her left shoulder, she tried not to disturb her new bunkmate, Gia.

Gia was an especially pretty girl, with the delicate features of the highborn and an imperious attitude to match. She'd made it clear that she did not approve of Sarah and refused to speak to her in English, even though Aiyako assured Sarah that she could.

Gia was also strangely cooperative when it came to dealing with the guards. As long as they treated her with deference, she treated them like favored pets, even going so far as to tattle on the other girls if they left their cots. Fondness for one's captors was a common problem with prisoners, Sarah knew—common enough that there was even a name for it: the Stockholm Syndrome. When the time came to make her move, Sarah would have to keep an eye out for Gia.

The tinny sound of footsteps on the gangway broke Sarah's concentration. She looked up and saw two men step into the room, one after the other. The first was one of the men who had brought her in here, the other was an ancient Japanese gentleman in red silk robes and a peaked hat. The first man carried a tray with five shot glasses and a decanter full of bluish-green liquid—probably creme de menthe and morphine, the same potion that the dead girl had been given. The older man carried a silk damask cloth and a small golden scepter.

The younger man set his tray down on one of the bunks and woke the girls. As each was pulled from her bed the old man poured a glass of liquid from the bottle, said a few words in Japanese, and lifted it to the girl's lips. Sarah noticed that none of the girls refused the drink when it was offered. She wondered if it had anything to do with the words the old man was saying.

Damn! She wished Aiyako could tell her what they were.

Finally, the man stopped at Sarah's cot. He took Gia out first and gave her the drink, then pulled Sarah to her feet. Sarah watched her bunkmate swallow obediently and decided not to put up a fuss. Without knowing what the old man was telling them, she had no way of knowing what her reaction should be. Was he assuring them that this was something good for them? Or perhaps telling them that refusal would mean death? She kept her back to the bunk as the old man said his incantation over her glass. She didn't want them to see how loose the bindings on her hands were.

The old man stepped up and Sarah opened her mouth, accepting the drink obediently even as her heart pounded. It was all she could do not to spit the poison out. Each of the girl's mouths had been checked after they'd taken the drink to make sure they'd swallowed, so that wasn't an option. As she felt the liquid trickle down her throat, she fought down a rising feeling of panic.

Don't worry, she told herself. *Everything's going according to the plan. As soon as they leave, you can get the Naloxone.*

The others would just have to wait for theirs.

The girls were put back in their bunks. Sarah hung back, hoping to be put on the outside, and it worked. Now she wasn't trapped next to the bulkhead behind Gia. Now, she had room to maneuver.

The men left. Sarah waited until she was sure they were out of sight and then rolled off the bed. She slipped her hands out of the ropes, lifted her dress, and removed the antidote while the other girls watched her with eyes wide.

"What you doing?" Aiyako asked.

Sarah glanced at her. "Trying to help you."

Gia looked around at the others and whispered something in Japanese.

Sarah looked at Aiyako. "What did she say?"

Aiyako blushed. "She say only a prostitute hides a weapon in her vagina."

Sarah turned and sneered at Gia. "Yeah, well you tell her that if she makes so much as a peep, I'll break her pretty little neck with my bare hands."

Gia didn't need an interpreter. Her hands flew up and covered her throat.

"Good," Sarah said. "Remember that."

Her hands shook as she tried to open the case. It was slippery, and Sarah had been lying on her side so long that her arms were weak. She pressed the latch, trying to pop it open, and the case fell out of her hands.

"Oh, shit."

She dropped to her knees and scrambled after the case; but on the metal floor, there was no friction to slow its progress. It rolled under the bunk and kept rolling until it hit the bulkhead. She flattened herself against the floor and dove after it.

There were footsteps in the hall. Sarah laced her fingers into the floor's gridwork and pulled her body forward. But the bunk was too low to slip under entirely; her legs were still sticking out. She hoped Gia would not give her away. Sarah reached out her right hand and tried to grab the case—two inches short. She inched her left hand forward and pulled again, still straining to reach with the right. Another inch to go. She felt a sharp pain in her head and realized her hair was caught on something. *Shit!* If her hair got yanked off, she'd be in big trouble.

But if she didn't reach the antidote, she'd be dead.

Clawing with both hands now, Sarah grabbed the grating and pulled again. She felt the pain for an instant longer and then something gave way. She stuck out her right hand and her fingers closed around the case.

Then Gia screamed.

The sound of heavy footsteps came crashing into the room. Sarah heard a man's voice and the other girls started screaming and babbling. Sarah popped open the case and grabbed the hypo. Whatever was going on behind her could be dealt with later. She needed the Naloxone and she needed it now. She stuck the safety cap in her mouth and yanked the needle free, turning her left hand over, ready to inject the drug.

Someone grabbed her ankles and pulled. The needle jumped, missing Sarah's arm. Sarah struggled, kicking her feet, as Naloxone dribbled down her arm. *Fuck!* She released the plunger and repositioned the needle. It was now or never. Jabbing the needle into her arm, she pushed the plunger and breathed a sigh of relief. Tomorrow, she'd have a hell of a bruise, but at least she'd be alive. As her ankles were grabbed a second time, Sarah shoved the hypo and the case through the floor grates.

Unless they pulled the bunks out, no one would ever find them under there.

The man who'd pulled Sarah out stood her up and pushed her back against the bunk. Sarah reached up and ran her hands over her hair to see how much of it was missing. Not enough that anyone would notice, she thought. The man's eyes widened when he saw her hands free. He took her by the shoulders and shook her.

Sarah closed her eyes and tried to remain calm. It was all she could do not to punch the guy. He was only about three inches taller than she was and slightly built—she could have decked him easily. But she couldn't afford to blow her cover. She hung her head and allowed herself to be berated.

The man continued to scream unintelligibly as Sarah waited for his temper to cool. She hoped he wasn't saying anything that required an answer—she couldn't understand a word. Then Gia came forward and tried to get his attention.

Oh God, thought Sarah, *I'm done for now.*

But instead of listening to Gia, the man slapped her, sending her reeling. She fell to the floor, cowering, and waited for someone to come to her rescue; but the others ignored her. An embarrassed minute later, she struggled to her feet and crawled back into her bunk alone.

Hitting Gia had taken some of the fury out of the man. He retied Sarah's hands, shoved her back into her cot, and left the room.

The other girls had been watching everything from the safety of their cots; now they peered at Gia and Sarah like owls. Sarah tugged at the ropes binding her wrists. She hadn't been prepared when her hands were tied. It would take longer to get out of the ropes again. She looked at Gia, curled up beside her and gave her a nudge.

"You okay?"

Gia's answer was in Japanese. A curt reply, delivered in bitter tones.

Sarah looked around. "What did she say?"

The girl in the opposite bunk leaned forward. "She say, you should have killed her before. It would have been better."

Chapter Thirty-six

August 23, 0420 hours,
Asuncion Island

Fifty amphib transports left the water and rolled up onto the sands of Iwo Jima. Sergeant Striker, Al Thomas, and the Flynn boys were the first to bail out. Jack followed Private Fowler over the side and hit the sand with his M-1 Garand at the ready. A barrage of bullets whizzed overhead. Striker ordered the men down.

Offshore, the Navy's battleships were lobbing salvos trying to soften up the interior. Jack lifted his chin and watched a Hellcat fly overhead, heading for the Jap strongholds on Mt. Suribachi. The smell of gunpowder and lead mixed with the awful stench of sulfur as the Marines dug in and waited for the signal to advance.

Fowler sifted a handful of sand through his fingers and shook his head. A country boy, he understood the value of good soil.

"This is the poorest soil I ever saw. What does anyone want to take an island like this for?"

Thomas shook his head. "That's war, boy. Trading real estate for men."

"When God made the world," Fowler said, "he must have taken all the dust and rubbish he had left over and put it here."

The last word was barely out of Fowler's mouth when a Jap bullet caught him in the back. The boy slumped forward and Thomas cried out for a medic. Striker seemed unfazed. In a war, death just happened. No sense wondering why.

Jack ducked as the Navy delivered another round of hellfire. How much longer could Kuribayashi hold out, he wondered. What would it take to rout the Japs from their tunnels? Then he heard a rumble. The tanks were rolling, turning their flamethrowers on the underground bunkers. Streams of liquid fire poured into the enemy strongholds. The Japs who weren't incinerated were buried alive under the tanks' treads. Striker narrowed his eyes and indicated the volcano in the distance.

"Lieutenant Shrier wants me to take a patrol up Suribachi in the morning. You ready, Sergeant?"

Jack nodded, thinking for the hundredth time how much Striker looked like John Wayne.

"Aye aye, sir."

The man seemed pleased. "All right. I'll get my men squared away and we'll be ready to move out at zero seven hundred. We'll rendezvous with that old Nip tank over there." He pointed.

Jack turned his head. He didn't see a tank. Couldn't see much of anything, really. He looked back and realized that Striker, too, was gone. What was happening? Where was he? He sat bolt upright and looked around, his heart pounding.

Hunter was asleep on his left, the hedgehogs wedged between them. They were still on Asuncion and the plane was still in one piece. Jack shook his head and thought about the movie he'd been dreaming about: *The Sands of Iwo Jima*. It wasn't the first time he'd pictured himself side-by-side with Duke Wayne and his misfit Marines; but it was the first time he'd dreamed about it so close to Iwo. Jack held his breath and listened for the wind to come up. When it didn't, he stepped into the cockpit.

In the west, the sky was clear and stars twinkled in the freshly scrubbed air. In the east, the horizon was beginning to glow. Jack checked his watch. Oh-four-twenty. He felt a surge of adrenaline—there was still time to get to Iwo before the sub! He stepped back to where Hunter was dozing and shook him.

"Get up! The storm's over."

Hunter opened his eyes. "What time is it?"

"Oh-four-twenty."

"Heard anything from Travis yet?"

"Nope."

Hunter sat up and stretched. "Let me take a quick look around to make sure the plane's okay."

"You think something might have happened to her in the storm?"

"Won't know till I fire her up."

Jack got into the co-pilot's seat and strapped himself in, ignoring the cramp in his stomach where food and water should have been.

Hunter opened his door and jumped into the cockpit.

"Everything looks good," he said. "Let's see if she'll fly."

He started the engines. A flock of shore birds rose up and scattered into the dim morning light, trying to escape the noise.

Hunter smiled. "So far so good."

"Yeah, but it was running before."

"Right. That's why we won't know how she's doing until we take her up."

"What if she's not fixed?"

"Then we won't get in the air. Or if we do, we'll come right back down."

"Oh."

Hunter put his helmet on and grinned. "Don't worry, Jack. This'll be fun."

"Oh yeah," Jack said, grimacing. "I forgot."

There wasn't enough room on the beach. They'd have to take off from the water. Hunter taxied across the damp sand into the leeward swells. Jack gripped the arm rests and looked out over the ocean. The water was as dark as death. The ground dropped away and suddenly they were floating. Hunter turned and looked at Jack.

"You ready for this?"

"Go for it."

Hunter pushed the throttle forward. As the Goose picked up speed, the plane began to shudder. It sank lower into the water. Jack felt like his eyeballs were going to bounce out of his head.

The plane kept going, the water now rising as high as

the window. The engines sounded like twin saw mills
and the vibrations were intense. Then the crate started
to lift. Higher in the water at first, then suddenly they
were soaring. Jack looked over at Hunter, his face beam-
ing, and realized the exhilaration a pilot must feel at a
time like this. A machine made of steel was flying like
a bird. And all because one man willed it to. He smiled
in admiration. It was a hell of a thing.

"How's it doing?"

Hunter checked the gauges. "So far so good."

"Does that mean we're on our way?"

"Looks like it."

Jack said a silent prayer. It wasn't too late. He was
on his way to Iwo.

"See if you can raise Travis, will you? I want him to
know we're on the way."

"Roger." Jack took the mic in his hand and tuned the
radio to the helmet's frequency.

"Boss? This is Jack. Do you read me? Over."

He waited. Nothing. He tried again.

"This is Jack, calling Travis. Do you read?"

He looked at Hunter and shook his head.

"That's okay," Hunter said. "We'll give them another
call in a—"

Sam's voice boomed out of the speaker. "Jack? This
is Sam. Where are you guys? Over."

Jack's heart leaped. "Sammy! We just left the island.
How's everything up there?"

"I can tell you about it later. Just get yourselves up
here on the double. The sub has arrived. Out."

Chapter Thirty-seven

When the engine vibrations stopped, Sarah knew they were getting out. She opened her eyes and looked around. Whether from the alcohol or from sheer exhaustion, she'd drifted off. Now, her senses were keen.

Without moving her head, she watched the men roll out of their bunks and prepare to leave. The other girls were either asleep or too groggy to be aware of what was going on. As the men padded back and forth from the head, she lay still, keeping her eyes narrowed.

There were twenty men in the bunks. If Sarah's observations were correct, that left twenty-five in the rest of the ship. Since he'd given the girls their cocktails, the old man hadn't shown up again. Sarah was still trying to figure out where he fit into the picture. If the girls were going to be some sort of sacrifice, they probably needed to have a holy man involved. Perhaps that was him.

Aiyako was snoring on the bunk across from Sarah, her mouth open, one leg flung over the side of the bunk. Sarah wished she could take the girls' vital signs. She'd packed enough Naloxone in Jennifer's kit to revive the rest of the girls when they got to the island, but it had to be administered within about two hours. If it wasn't, the girls' central nervous systems might be too weak to revive.

And where was Tomomi?

The men were returning from the showers, putting their clothes on. Sarah watched as they opened their foot

lockers and removed brightly colored tunics and swords.
If she didn't know better, she'd say they looked like
samurai.

Was it possible? One of the men stepped up next to
the girls' beds and leered at them. Sarah tensed, remem-
bering the groper; but another of the men barked an
order and the man returned to his bunk.

When all the men were suited up, the old man came
into the room and said a few solemn words. Then the
girls were dragged from their bunks, groggy and placid.
Sarah feigned stupor as she was taken from her bed and
thrown over a man's shoulder.

This was it, she thought. Either the team was out there
or it wasn't.

And if they're not, then everything is up to me.

The men carried the girls down the companionway
and up two flights of metal stairs, through a hatch, and
finally topside. Sarah hung limply over the man's shoulder as they exited the sub and a bracing wind hit her
face.

A Zodiac—an inflatable watercraft—was tethered to
the sub's superstructure. It had a sleek V-shape with two
benches in the center and an outboard motor in back.
Seating seven girls and their captors would be a tight fit.
As Sarah was set down in her seat, she noticed one of
the other girls starting to rouse. Good. That gave her
some cover. She opened her eyes and looked around.

The sun was almost up. Off in the east, the horizon
glowed and the sky was a pinkish gray. A quarter mile
away to the west, a strip of land hugged the water. An
island, but which one? There were hundreds if not thousands of islands in the South Pacific. Sarah wished she
knew how long they'd been underwater and how fast
they'd been going. At least then she'd be able to narrow
down the possibilities.

The Zodiac was untethered and the man at the stern
fired up the outboard motor. Sarah strained to see the
thin slice of land that lay just ahead. A second Zodiac
lay on the broad stretch of black sand directly in their
path; at either end of the beach were pillboxlike struc-

tures; on the southern end of the island was a mountain.
She squinted. No. Not a mountain. A volcano.

Seconds later, the inflatable craft hit the beach and
the girls tumbled forward. The man at the helm jumped
out and he and several men waiting on the beach pulled
the Zodiac up onto the sand. Sarah managed to keep
herself upright, but sagged as she was pulled from the
boat. No sense making this easy for anybody.

When they were all on shore, Sarah looked around.
Most of the girls were awake, if groggy, so her observations went unnoticed. On her left was the bulk of the
island, including three airstrips, on her right was a narrow path that led to the top of the volcano. Sarah saw
more men waiting for them there, all of them in the
same samurai getups she'd seen on the men in the crew's
quarters; but in addition to the wicked-looking swords
at their sides, these men carried AK-47s. What did it
mean, she wondered. What were samurai doing here?

The men formed the girls in a line and they stumbled
along the path toward the volcano. Sarah wrinkled her
nose. The place smelled like sulfur—probably a result of
all the volcanic activity here. She stepped haphazardly
along the path, trying not to seem too lucid as she
searched the area.

Where, she wondered, was the rest of TALON Force?

Chapter Thirty-eight

**August 23, 0530 hours,
airfield #1, Iwo Jima**

Beneath the rapidly lightening sky, the second Zodiac skimmed over the gray water, closing rapidly on the beach. The sub was anchored about five hundred yards off shore, its sail sticking proudly out of the water. Sam had been right—it was a Z V class. Travis lifted his visor and watched the latest boatload through his binoculars. His suite's battery array was low on power; he didn't want to use the BSD any more than was absolutely necessary. As he brought the Zodiac into focus, he smiled.

"There they are. Stan, Jen, you in on this? Over."

Stan was the first to answer. "Got 'em in my sights. Which one's Sarah, can you tell?"

Jen had taken up her position behind the pillbox on the far side of the runway. She was the closest of the group to the invasion beach where the men were coming ashore. From her vantage point, she didn't need binoculars to count the bogeys. Jen's voice was like a whisper in Travis's ear.

"She's the second one back from the bow on the port side."

Travis reached up and pressed his transmitter. "Stan? How many are up where you are? Over."

Stan was hunkered down on the far side of the volcano, his brilliant suit blending flawlessly into the surrounding rock and ash. He was using a UAV to help him navigate. Lucky for them, Mt. Suribachi had been belching up a steady stream of smoke all morning. It gave Stan cover for the UAV and he could see through it with his thermal viewer.

"Thirty-two Japs. Over."

"How many of them have weapons?"

"All of them."

"What kind of ordnance?"

"AK-47s and samurai swords—who knows what else under their tunics. I don't think these sons of Nippon are expecting any trouble, though; they don't look too bright. Over."

"Even an idiot can cause trouble with a Kalashnikov. How's your power supply holding out?"

"Less than half a charge on the battery. Between the heat and the camo, the suit's sucking up the juice. It'll last maybe another hour, tops."

"That should be enough. Once these tangos are all out of the sub, we'll begin executing the plan. Jen? What's your status?"

"Two thirds power on my suite and I'm not using the BSD. That should last me. Over."

"Good. Hold your fire until we're sure everyone's on shore. When I give the signal, we'll go forward. Travis out."

Travis hunkered down and watched as the seven girls were pulled from the rubber craft and marched up the hillside toward the top of Mt. Suribachi. As they moved forward, they lurched and stumbled—no doubt drugged as the dead girl had been. Sarah, too, did her fair share of stumbling but, Travis noted, she also seemed to be searching the area with her eyes. The Zodiacs had gone back to the sub for more men—they wouldn't start shooting for a while. Travis wriggled back down into the tunnel to talk to Sam.

Sam was sitting in the underground bunker, his broken ankle propped up on a rucksack, his PowerBook open in his lap. With it, he was able to follow the goings-on above ground; but the satellite dish had been lost in the storm, severely limiting the power of their command and control. On the ground next to him was a sub aqua Glock, a "one-shot, one-kill" 9mm handgun. Designed to be fired underwater, it had the added advantage of being light enough for Sam to hold for long periods without tiring.

When Travis stepped through the door, Sam didn't even look up.

"They just brought in the girls."

"I heard."

"I'd like to tell Sarah where we are. Any way you could send a signal from here to reprogram her implant?"

Sam nodded slowly. "I could do that."

"Have you heard anything more from the plane?"

"Not since they called."

"Did you tell them the sub was here?"

He nodded again. "They said they'd get here as fast as they could."

Travis ran a hand down his face. His impulse was to tell Sam to snap out of it; but Sam had been looking forward to playing a key role in this operation. Now, with his ankle broken and the satellite dish lost, he was stuck down here away from all the action. In retrospect, maybe giving him a weapon had been an insult.

"How long will it take you to get Sarah for me?"

"Couple of minutes."

"I'm heading up topside. Let me know when it's done."

0537 hours

Jen squatted behind the pillbox, watching as another Zodiac full of men ran up onto the beach. That made forty-one men so far. How many more were there? She wished Jack and Hunter would get there. She'd feel a lot better about their chances with two more on their side.

She snapped down her BSD and watched Sarah; she and the others were almost to the top of Mt. Suribachi now. How much longer was Travis going to wait? The men standing around the girls were all in ceremonial costume—silk tunics in a rainbow of colors with head coverings that hung down the sides of their faces like dog's ears. Their appearance would be almost comical if it wasn't for the weapons they carried. Jennifer patted the M-16 in her lap.

Stan would be the designated sniper for this assignment. He was the surest shot of the three of them and had the best vantage point behind the volcano. Once Travis was satisfied that all the men had come out of the sub, Stan would begin picking off the guards around the girls to try and break them up and see how they would react. This wasn't a regular army they were fighting; there were no platoons or divisions, no uniforms to show who was in charge. Taking down a few samurai would force them to assemble themselves along their chain of command. For all the teasing Jack took about quoting *The Art of War,* Travis himself had taken the strategy straight out of Sun Tzu's play book.

"Agitate him and ascertain the pattern of his movement."

Once the girls were no longer the focus of attention, the team was hoping that Sarah would get them herded up and out of the way. That was one big advantage she had over the enemy; Sarah knew Travis's moves, the bad guys didn't. Unfortunately, she wouldn't know until the shooting started that the team was there. Jen hoped Sarah wouldn't try something on her own.

The first Zodiac was in the water again, its sixty horsepower motor whining as it left the beach and headed back toward the sub. Jen figured it had to be pretty close to empty; the ship only carried something like fifty men. She hoped this would be the last trip. She didn't want to wait much longer.

"Jen? This is Travis. How's it looking from over there? Over."

She reached up and touched her transmitter. "Eight more men on the beach and the first Zodiac's just headed back for more. The second one's still tied up at the sub."

"What's that take us up to?"

"Forty-one including the guy piloting the boat."

"Roger that. Listen, Sam's figured out a way to remotely reprogram Sarah's implant chip so we can let her know we're here."

"Excellent." Jen closed her eyes. This was good news.

"There's just one problem."

"What?"

"Without the dish, we're going to have to have a clear line of sight to send the signal."

"No problem. I can send it from here."

"That's what I was thinking. But we're also going to need more power. The program's got to be sent in a concentrated burst to override the implant's current program. If you send it, we're going to have to use your battery array. It'll drop your suite time way down."

Jen nodded, peering at the girls huddled now at the rim of the volcano. "How soon can he do it?"

"Any time you're ready."

"Let's go for it."

"Sam's going to need for you to make some changes in your setup and then he'll route the signal through your helmet. After that, we should be able to contact her. Over."

"Roger that. Sam, what do you need?"

0544 hours

Stan had his XM-29 propped up on the volcano's edge as he waited for Travis's signal. He had fifty rounds of armor-piercing ammo in the magazine and four 20mm grenades in the launcher under the barrel. When the shit came down, these motherfuckers wouldn't know what hit them.

He hunkered down over the weapon and drew a bead on his first most likely target, a beefy guy standing to Sarah's left.

"Pfft," he whispered and mimed pulling the trigger. "Got you."

After that, he figured he'd take down the guard on the other side of the girls, then maybe one of the tangos standing near the pathway farther down. The first shot would confuse them, the second one would scare them. It would take the third one to convince them they were under attack. Then, the fun would start. The point wasn't to decimate their ranks, but to get the girls out of harm's way and put the bad guys on the defensive. If they were smart, they'd lay down their weapons and make it easy for themselves. If not, well, a SEAL never minded having to do things the hard way.

A drop of sweat snaked down the side of Stan's face and ran under his chin. The heat up here was almost unbearable. The ground was hot and the sulfur-tinged steam was making his eyes water while it turned his stomach.

Thank God for his battle ensemble. In addition to providing nearly flawless camouflage, the suit had Health Status Sensors woven into the fabric that monitored Stan's temperature, blood pressure, and bodily integrity. If Stan was hurt, the HSS would signal the microsensors in the fabric and the suit would respond. Working with the Automatic Trauma Med pack, it could close a wound, apply pressure to stop bleeding, and maintain body temperature and fluid levels to keep the wearer from going into shock before help arrived. It didn't make you immortal, but it sure made going into combat easier.

So why wasn't it keeping him any cooler?

He lifted his head slightly and watched as one of the Zodiacs left the sub and started for shore.

Man, that better be the last load.

He reached up and pressed his transmitter.

"Travis? Stan. How much longer till we rock and roll? I'm cooked about medium well up here. Over."

"Not long. Sam's reprogramming Sarah's implant so we can tell her to keep her head down."

"Good idea. Hope it works. Out."

Stan checked the readout from his suite. The battery array was down to one-quarter charge. The suit was draining the battery, trying to keep him cool. He could turn off the Trauma Med Pack and save power that way; but without it, he'd have to take up another post, and there weren't any cooler ones any place close. No. If the charge got too much lower, he'd just turn off the camo and hope the enemy didn't spot him.

He heard Travis's voice in his ear.

"Sarah? This is Travis. Can you hear me?"

Stan watched Sarah's face for a reaction. Nothing.

"Sarah, I know you can't do anything to give yourself away, but I want you to know we're here and what we're up to. First, there's only Stan, Jennifer, Sam, and me on the island. Jack and Hunter are on their way, but we can't count on them. Jen's behind the pillbox you saw when you got off the Zodiac. I'm at the north end of the airstrip about midway between the leeward and windward sides. Stan's on the other side of the volcano."

At the instant Travis gave Stan's position away, he saw Sarah's eyes flicker up. Had she heard what Travis said, or was she merely watching the steam rise?

"If you can hear me, do something to let us know. I need to know you're with us."

Sarah's knees suddenly buckled and she went down on the ground. The guards rushed over and yanked her roughly to her feet. Stan smiled.

"Good girl," Travis said. "I knew this would work. Now, listen carefully. We're going to need all the help we can get."

Chapter Thirty-nine

Jack strained forward in his seat, willing the plane to go faster. They had to make it to Iwo in time. They had to! He closed his eyes and said a silent prayer.

"You okay?"

Jack nodded. "How much farther?"

"Just under a hundred nauticals. We should be there in another twenty minutes or so. Can you see anything?"

Jack shook his head. "Not yet. The damned clouds are too low."

"How about with the thermal viewer?"

Jack flipped his visor down and shook his head. "Still nothing. I don't think it's in range yet."

"All right. Call Travis. Tell him we're on a north by northwest heading. We should be there in fifteen minutes. Ask him what kind of help he's going to need."

"Got it." Jack grabbed the mic. "Boss? This is Jack. Do you read me? Over."

There was nothing but static. He glanced at Hunter and pressed the transmit button again.

"Travis? Sam? This is Jack. Do you read? Over."

The two of them waited. Neither one could hear anything but the drone of the engines. Then, faintly, a voice came through the static.

"This is Travis. I read you loud and clear. Where are you? Over."

Jack and Hunter cheered.

Jack held the mic to his mouth to try and cancel out the noise from the plane.

"We're a hundred nautical miles from Iwo coming in on a north by northwest heading. Hunter says we'll be there in fifteen minutes. What's your status up there? Where's the sub?"

"Sub's offshore. We've got forty-one tangos here and seven girls, including Sarah. Another boatload of unfriendlies is about to land. Any chance you can get here faster? Over."

Hunter shook his head. "I doubt it; but tell him I'll try."

"Hunter says he'll try. Think you can wait that long?"

"Negative. We're running out of time. Sorry, Jack. Looks like we're going to have to start the party without you."

Jack took a deep breath. "Roger that. Black Jack out."

Chapter Forty

Sarah stood at the north rim of the volcano, looking down across the island. The sun was just coming up over the eastern horizon, illuminating the island like a spot-light. There was the pillbox where Jen waited. There was the airstrip—Travis would be there somewhere. Behind her, Stan was waiting for the signal to go. It wouldn't be long now.

Her hands were finally free. She'd been working on the bindings since this morning and had gotten them off after giving Travis her signal. She still had her hands behind her back, but now the rope was in them, not tied around them.

On her right, Aiyako swayed drunkenly from side to side, trying to stay on her feet. Gia and two of the other girls lay in a stupor on the ground beyond her. The other two girls were on either end of the line, still on their feet, but wobbly. When the shooting started, Sarah's first job would be to get them all down on the ground. Then, when it was safe, she'd move them around to the far side of the mountain until the samurai were routed. The biggest obstacle she could see at this point was the guard hovering nearby. Ordinarily, he'd be a natural first shot for Stan; but if he got too close, Stan might pick another target. If that happened, Sarah would have to take him out herself.

Her grip on the rope tightened.

*　　*　　*

Travis crept away from the tunnel and into position. With his brilliant suit activated, he was all but invisible as he moved across the lichen-covered flatland toward a rocky outcropping near the footpath. The last boatload of tangos was on the beach. He pulled down his BSD and brought them into focus. Five men in all; four of them samurai. The fifth man sat in the bow, his arms crossed, the look on his face haughty and defiant. He wore a large headdress that flared out at the sides like a clipper ship, a red silk robe, and silk pants. When he stepped out of the boat, the men on shore knelt, bowing until their foreheads touched the ground. Travis pressed his transmitter.

"The head honcho has arrived."

"Roger," Jen whispered. "I see him."

"Roger that," said Stan.

"Keep your targets in sight and hold your fire. We'll go on my signal. Out."

The leader was about halfway up the path now. Travis lifted his chin and watched the man proceed toward the volcano's mouth. In front of him walked an old man in a red robe and a pointed cap. Behind him were the four men who'd accompanied him in the Zodiac, carrying a table. Along the path, whenever they passed, the others prostrated themselves.

"Sam? Can you see any of this? Over."

"Not clearly. I saw the shore and a boat a minute ago."

"Did you see the bogeys inside?"

"Sort of. There was a guy in front with a big head. Over."

"It's a hat. Hold on, let me see if I can steady this thing." Travis rested his chin in his hand and tried to hold still while the scene in front of him beamed from his helmet down to Sam.

"I see it now. Whoa. That's weird."

"What?"

"The way he's dressed. He looks like a shogun—a Japanese warlord."

"I know what a shogun is. What the hell's he doing here?"

"Good question."

"All right, thanks Sam. Out."

Travis squinted at the man walking slowly up the pathway. A shogun, huh? Now, what did that mean? He pressed his transmitter.

"Stan? Travis. Sam says this guy coming up the hill is a shogun. Over."

"That would explain the reception he's getting. Over."

"Roger. He's also the guy who's going to be able to tell us what the deal is. When the shooting starts, leave him be."

"Roger."

"Jen?"

"A shogun—I heard. Sarah and the girls are awfully close to that volcano's edge. One false move and they're over the top."

"Roger that. Stan? Fire when ready."

"Roger."

Chapter Forty-one

When the first tango went down, no one but Sarah seemed to notice. As the man fell, she grabbed Aiyako's arm and pulled her down. The guard in front of them looked startled and took a step forward. Sarah turned and heard another *Pfft!* A blossom of red burst open on the guard's chest and he hit the ground. Sarah grabbed the girls and pushed them one after another face down into the ash.

The men along the pathway still hadn't noticed that anything was wrong; but nearer the top, the bogeys were beginning to scatter. Then a third tango bit the dirt and the place started swarming like an anthill with a big shoe hovering above it.

Sarah went down the row, untying the girls' hands, trying to keep her head down. The samurai had their weapons unslung and were forming into groups; so far, they'd left the girls alone. Gia's hands were almost free when Sarah heard a burst of suppressing fire from the far side of the volcano and heard Stan's voice in her ear.

"Sarah! Behind you!"

She turned. A samurai in a bright green tunic was almost on top of her. There was no time to prepare. As he took her arm and pulled her off her feet, Sarah willed herself to relax.

As your opponent moves, move with him.

The man, expecting resistance, staggered back. Sarah put her hands against his chest and pushed off, regained her balance, then swung her leg around and cut his feet out from under him. He went down hard.

The other guards were getting bold now. But they were unarmed; as they advanced on the girls, Sarah attacked.

There were two of them. Sarah didn't wait for them to make a move. She grabbed the first man's arm and yanked him off balance, then shoved him back into the other. On the slippery ground, the first man went down easily. The other staggered, but didn't fall. Instead, he crouched, advancing on her with arms out, elbows bent—a classic martial arts stance. Sarah assumed her own pose and waited for him to make the first move. She wanted to see if he knew what he was doing. If he didn't, his first move would give him away.

The man took two quick steps forward and kicked, aiming for Sarah's head. She ducked in time to feel the force of the blow pass overhead.

Okay, so he was good.

But he was fighting uphill on loose ground, and he still didn't know who Sarah was. To him, she was just a Japanese school girl who'd been lucky enough to dodge his kick in time. He was about to get the surprise of his life.

The guard's foot hadn't even touched the ground before Sarah attacked. She closed the distance between them in two quick steps, flexed her right leg, and kicked, catching him in the forehead with her heel. As he staggered, Sarah delivered three quick body blows. The man doubled over, a look of shock and disbelief on his face. Sarah yanked him forward and gave him a chop behind the head. He went down like a sack of potatoes.

Bullets were flying all around them now. Sarah had to get the girls off the volcano.

"Aiyee!"

One of the other guards had Gia. Sarah grabbed the rope and leaped onto his back, looping the length of hemp around his neck. The man bucked and twirled, trying to shake her off; but Sarah held fast. Holding onto him with her knees, she tightened the rope around his neck until she felt his windpipe crack. The man staggered forward a few steps and collapsed.

Sarah pushed away from her adversary and rolled to the side, breathing hard. Beside her, Gia seemed stunned.

"Thank you," she whispered.

"Sure," Sarah panted. "No problem."

The two of them hugged the ground as a burst of automatic weapons fire sounded behind them. Sarah saw another man charge up the hill. Dodging bullets, waving a sword, he was coming straight toward the girls.

"Banzai!"

Sarah scrambled to her feet and threw herself in front of him. It was like trying to stop a train. He plowed into her and kept going. But he'd been derailed. As he continued forward toward the lip of the volcano, his arms wheeled and his feet flew. He teetered on the brink, trying in vain to regain his balance. The sword dropped from his hand and slid down the inside of the steaming caldera. Sarah held her breath.

Then the unthinkable happened.

Aiyako reached out and grabbed the man's hand. And the two of them tumbled into the volcano.

Chapter Forty-two

When Aiyako fell over the edge, Stan was having his own problems. The tangos were returning fire and the suit was hotter than ever. He laid down a burst of suppressing fire and ducked back down to check his battery array. Not even an eighth of a charge left! He couldn't keep draining his reserves like this. He had to choose: stay cool or stay camouflaged. A Hobson's choice if there ever was one. Without the camo, he could still fight; but if he got any hotter, he'd have to move—maybe even without the benefit of camouflage at the rate the suit was using juice. No, there was no choice. The camo had to go.

He turned the brilliant suit off and immediately felt the difference. Without two systems draining the battery's power, the ATMP could do its job. Seconds later, he was cool as a glass of iced tea on the Fourth of July.

Unfortunately, he was also as visible. As soon as Stan raised his head over the ridge, a cry went up from the bogeys on the other side and bullets began to fly. He was pinned down.

The tangos had split themselves into two groups. The first one was still trying to hold the hill. The second had formed a phalanx around the shogun and was ushering him back to the beach. As Travis watched, the mob passed by only fifty yards in front of him.

Damn! He wished he didn't need to keep the shogun

alive. But who else in the group would know the reason they were here? The aim of this mission wasn't just to rescue the girls, it was to rescue them *and* find out why they'd been kidnapped.

Still, that didn't mean he couldn't scare the guy a little.

He sighted a tango at the back of the group and squeezed the trigger. The XM-29 bucked in his hand. One bad boy down.

The group started moving more quickly, but the men around the shogun held their positions.

Loyal bastards.

Travis decided to pick off another one.

Another shot. Another tango down. The shogun's men were getting nervous. Three of them knelt and returned fire. Travis ducked behind the rocks and heard the report from Jen's XM-29.

"Good girl."

She'd seen what he was up to and was giving him some cover. The enemy still didn't know how many adversaries they were up against. The more directions the bullets came from, the more men they'd figure were out there.

Travis peered over the rocks and watched the shogun's group. They'd splintered again. One group had taken up positions behind some rocks next to the pathway, the other was still working as a human shield, moving the shogun toward the beach. Travis's heart sank. With so few men around to protect him, the shogun must have guessed that he wasn't a target.

It'd be so easy just to take him out, Travis thought. It might even force the rest to lay down their weapons. But he couldn't do it. Not if he wanted to complete his mission.

A shot whizzed by his head and pinged off the rock to his right. Travis ducked. That hadn't come from the shogun's men. He peered up in the direction of the volcano.

A group of about ten men had dug themselves in and were firing on Stan's position. The girls seemed to be out of the line of fire, but Sarah was scrambling toward the edge.

"Stan? Travis. What's your status up there?"

"My suit's almost drained. I had to switch off the camo. Fucking bogeys have me pinned."

"Roger. I'm on my way. Jen? Hold these guys while I give Stan some backup."

"Roger."

Travis tucked his head down and started creeping toward the hill. The ricochet off the rock had been a lucky shot; his suit was still working beautifully. Without his visor down, he might not even have seen his own arm as it passed in front of his face.

Then he heard Jen's voice.

"Travis, this is Jen. We've got a tango in the hole. Repeat. One of the bad guys just went into a tunnel."

"Which one?"

"It's a long one, but it leads to the bunker."

"Shit." If a tango got to their base camp, he'd have a hostage and the means to screw up their command and control.

"There's a feeder tunnel near me," Jennifer said. "If I go now, I can get him. Over."

Travis glanced down at the beach. The shogun and his men were almost to the boat. If Jen left her position, they'd have no one opposing them as they got into the Zodiac and made their escape. He could take her place, but Stan needed help. He searched the sky for the plane. The cloud cover was too thick to see anything. *Shit!* Where were Hunter and Jack? He pressed his transmitter.

"Do it."

Chapter Forty-three

August 23, 0601 hours,
the underground tunnels, Iwo Jima

Jen landed feet first as surface debris rained down on her head. Seen through the BSD, the warm walls of the tunnel were white, the way in front of her a dark and shapeless void. She crouched, holding the XM-29 in her hands, and made her way forward.

She'd reconnoitered this tunnel yesterday. A hundred feet ·in, it linked up with a small bunker, then jogged sharply left for about fifty feet before joining up with the main passageway. The tango's tunnel had no bunker between it and the main tunnel. If he went left, he'd run straight into Jennifer. If he went right, he'd stumble into the team's base camp.

And Sam.

Jennifer hurried forward. She made it to the bunker and turned left. The ground was littered with WWII vintage ration cans and broken weapons and it slowed her progress as she closed in on the main tunnel.

She checked the readout on her visor. The tango had gone underground two minutes ago. She'd been following him for half that time. Which direction was he headed? There was no guarantee he'd even made it to the main passageway. Maybe just getting out of the line of fire had been enough for him. Maybe he was just hunkered down in the hole where he'd jumped. Unfortunately, Jen didn't have the luxury of staying in one spot. She needed to rout the enemy and do it fast.

At the entrance to the main tunnel, Jen squatted down

and peered around the corner. Her camo was still working pretty well, and unless her adversary had truly ex-
traordinary night vision, he wouldn't be able to see her.
He might have a flashlight, though, and that could be a
problem if he hit her right in the eye. The images the
BSD gave her were beamed directly onto her retina.
Anything that overloaded the optic nerve would wipe
the images clean.

Jen decided to call Sam and tell him what was
happening.

"Sam?" she whispered. "This is Jen. I'm in the main
tunnel, following a bad guy who might be headed your
way. Do you read? Over."

No response. Jennifer knew Sam's reception had been
bad since he and Stan had brought the equipment back
from the boat. Was he just not responding or was the
system down?

"Sam? Jen. Do you read?"

Still no answer. Jen couldn't waste any more time.
She'd get to the bunker soon enough. Sam could take
care of himself. She hoped. In the meantime, she had to
make sure their tango didn't get away.

Chapter Forty-four

August 23, 0604 hours,
on the northern rim of Mt. Suribachi, Iwo Jima

The ground was almost unbearably hot. As Sarah inched forward, she thought her shirt would burst into flame.

"Help me!"

Aiyako had fallen into the mouth of the volcano, but managed to stop herself from tumbling into its fiery abyss. Considering she was under the influence, Sarah was amazed that Aiyako had been able to stop herself. Not so the man she'd tried to save. Momentum and mass had combined to hurtle him down the rocky interior of the caldera and into the steaming cauldron below. His screams had been horrible, but brief.

Sarah peered over the lip of the caldera and was driven back as a blast of sulfurous steam hit her face. She doubled up, retching, and wondered how on earth she was going to get Aiyako out of there.

The rope was still in her hand.

"Aiyako!" she yelled over the thrum of the volcano. "I've got an idea! I'm going to throw the rope down to you. Grab hold of it and I'll pull you up! Can you do that?"

Aiyako's voice rose up from the mist. "Yes."

Sarah wrapped the end of the rope around her palm.

"All right. On the count of three, I'll toss it down to you and you grab it! One . . . two . . ." Sarah took a deep breath. "Three!"

She sprang up and threw the rope at Aiyako. The hemp twisted and bounced in the humidity, then came to rest about a foot from where Aiyako's fingers were dug into the ash.

"Reach out and grab it," Sarah coaxed. "Go on."

"I, I afraid!"

"Do it!" Sarah barked. "Before both of us get cooked!"

Aiyako pulled her hand away from the ash and grabbed for the lifeline. Sarah felt her body jerk forward as the girl's weight was added to the rope.

"All right. Hang on!"

Sarah dug the heel of her free hand into the ground and pushed, using her hips as a lever to bring Aiyako to the surface.

"Try and walk up," she yelled. "See if you can get a toehold!"

Aiyako scrabbled, sending rock and ash careening down the inside of the cone. Sarah pulled harder, trying not to take the caustic air too deeply into her lungs. Not much farther.

Come on, Aiyako. You can do it!

An instant later, Aiyako's head and shoulders rose up over the edge. Sarah lunged forward and grabbed her arm, dragging her back over the edge and down to where the other girls were waiting.

Sarah went down on her knees, panting and sweaty. Her hands and face were burned where she'd pressed them against the hot rocks. Aiyako sucked her burned fingers, crying softly. Sarah wiped a hand across her face. Thank God that was over.

Then a bullet whizzed by her head. She lurched forward and threw herself over the girls.

"Get down!"

Bullets continued to bite the ground around them, sending bits of rock and ash flying into the air.

"Sarah!" It was Travis. "Get the girls out of there! You're in the middle of a fire fight!"

Travis watched Sarah herd the girls away from the bogeys who were advancing up the hill toward Stan. Once they were out of the way, he'd be able to give Stan some relief.

With Sarah's encouragement, the girls huddled behind a rocky outcropping away from the action. Travis drew down on the nearest samurai and pulled the trigger.

A burst of fire erupted from the XM-29. One tango went down, another dropped his weapon and rolled on the ground, screaming. From his position behind the volcano, Stan got off a few more shots and the samurai took cover.

One of the tangos got behind a rock and returned fire in Travis's direction. He hugged the ground as bullets bit the dirt all around him. Out in the open like this, it was dangerous to fire his weapon; but this part of the island was bare of cover and there had been no other place he'd had a clear line of sight.

Fortunately, with three more tangos out of commission, Stan was able to go back on the offensive. Without return fire, the guy pinning Travis down lost interest and turned around.

Travis turned back and looked at the beach. The shogun and his men were getting into the Zodiac. He raised up on one elbow and took aim at the boat. One shot. If he could hit the inflatable, it'd be useless.

And if he hit the shogun, he'd be screwed.

He lowered the barrel and watched helplessly as the men piled into the Zodiac and took off.

Then Travis heard a buzzing overhead. He squinted up at the clouds and saw a plane approaching from the southeast. At the same time, Jack's voice spoke in his ear.

"Travis? This is Jack! We have you on visual. What can we do for you? Over."

Travis grinned.

"The shogun and his guards are heading back to the sub. Can you stop them?"

"Affirmative."

"The guy in the headdress is the shogun. We need to take him alive. Repeat. Bring the big fish in alive. Out."

Chapter Forty-five

Jen pressed her back against the tunnel wall, listening. She'd been in the main passageway for seven minutes now and had not yet acquired the bogey. Now, she waited behind another bend in the tunnel to see if she could tell where he was.

She'd already passed the feeder tunnel where he'd entered the system and found it empty. From that point, there were only two directions he could have gone in. One was the direction she'd come from, the other was down toward the bunker—and Sam. She took a deep breath, trying to stay calm. Her heart was pounding in her ears and her hands were slick with sweat. Without fresh air to breathe, the tunnel seemed to be closing in on her.

Something cracked. A footstep. Then another. Someone was moving cautiously through the tunnel up ahead. But was it the tango? Sam was still up there somewhere. What if he'd left the bunker and come this way? She couldn't just turn the corner and fire blindly. She had to be sure.

Jen crouched slowly and crab walked toward the bend in the wall. Her weapon was up, her finger on the trigger. When she stuck her head around the corner, she'd have only a split second to make the call: friend or foe. She stopped. Whoever it was had taken another step. She wished she could call Sam and confirm it was him, but she didn't want to give her position away. If this was her man, she'd need the element of surprise on her side.

Jen licked her lips. It was now or never. She stepped out around the corner and swung her weapon out.

A shot rang out, nicking a piece of the wall next to her ear. Jen hit the deck and returned fire. A burst of automatic weapons fire echoed in the tunnel. Jen jerked her body back around the corner and heard footsteps running away from her. She swung her weapon around the corner and let loose a burst of fire. The footsteps continued as the samurai ran deeper into the belly of the earth.

Jennifer pressed her transmitter.

"Sam, this is Jen! Do you read me? Over!"

Nothing. Jen took a deep breath. Damn! What was the problem? Was it her transmitter?

"Travis, this is Jen. Do you read? Over."

"This Travis. I can read you Jen, but you're real faint. What's the problem?"

Jen pressed her receiver. "I think my battery array's about dead; I have to conserve power. Call Sam and tell him I'm on my way."

"I'm barely reading you, Jen. Conserve your power till I can get to you. Travis out."

Jennifer shook her head. "No! You've got to call Sam! Tell him I'm coming! Over."

Travis didn't answer. There was no more time to wait. She had to move on. Jen removed her finger from behind her ear. It came away sticky.

Damn! There was blood on her hand. Lots of it. And now that she noticed it, her arm felt strange, too. She searched herself for a wound and found it just below her right elbow. *Shit!* The bullet must have passed right between the bones of her forearm and out the other side.

She watched as the suit's fabric tightened, trying to stanch the flow of blood. With its power low, the ATMP was barely strong enough to keep it to a trickle. And the BSD ran off the same power source. If she directed all the power to the suit, she'd have to stumble the rest of the way blind. Then again, if she turned the suit off she might bleed to death.

She squeezed her hand into a fist and wiggled her fingers. They felt strange, but everything still worked. She'd take care of this later. Right now, she had a bogey to catch.

Chapter Forty-six

Sarah grabbed Gia under her armpits and dragged her along the rocky ground toward the base of the volcano where three of the other girls were huddled. Aiyako's hands were badly burned and in need of medical attention. The others were suffering from varying degrees of heat exhaustion. But heat was the least of their worries. The girls' drowsiness had intensified and it was getting harder and harder to keep them awake. If Sarah didn't get the Naloxone into them soon, they'd all lapse into comas and die. She propped Gia up against a rock and hurried back to rescue another girl.

Bullets whizzed up ahead as Sarah scrambled along the cone toward the girls' position. She lifted her head and saw the place where the tangos were firing on Stan. From the number of volleys coming from the rocks, she could tell there were fewer tangos than there had been; but they'd grown bold in the last few minutes. Running from rock to rock, firing both uphill at Stan and down on Travis's position, they had advanced up the cone on the far side, driving Stan back down the south side of the volcano.

She wondered why they hadn't fired at the girls.

As if to answer her question, a bullet whizzed overhead and struck the ground ten feet in front of her. Sarah flattened herself against the ground and waited. The bullet hadn't come from the tangos who'd been firing on Stan. Somewhere below her, someone new had decided to join the fight.

"Sarah, this is Travis. You've got a bad guy behind you, moving up fast. Hold still. I'm going to try and pick him off before he gets to you."

Sarah nodded, but didn't answer. She didn't want to risk raising her head to reach the implant. She closed her eyes and waited.

She could hear the man's grunts now, felt the tremors in the ground as he scampered up the hill toward her. A volley of shots rang out from Travis's position. She heard an *Oof!* as he hit the ground.

Get him, Travis.

Then she heard a burst of stuttering fire she recognized as the report from an AK-47. Sarah rested her cheek on the ground, unmindful of the heat. Somehow, the prospect of being shot in the back had taken her mind off getting burned.

The ground around her feet erupted as bullets sprayed the rocks, scattering black volcanic sand, ash, and dust in all directions. Too close for comfort. This guy was out for blood. She heard him moving. He was coming her way.

Why wasn't Travis firing? Had he been hit? Sarah felt sick. What if Travis had been taken out and she was still lying here when the guy showed up? It was the worst way to go, she thought. Shot at point blank range without putting up a fight. She swallowed. She could hear the guy panting as he made his way toward her.

She had to do something, at least for the girls. If this guy killed her, there'd be no hope for them at all. Her mind was in high gear, trying to come up with some way to get the girls to safety before this guy overtook their position. But no matter how hard she tried, she couldn't come up with anything. She closed her eyes and waited for the bullet.

When it came, it wasn't the stutter of an AK-47, but the breathy report of an XM-29. Sarah opened her eyes and saw the samurai, his eyes wide, drop to his knees and keel forward. His head landed only inches from her flank.

"Sarah, Travis here. Thanks for holding still. I was waiting for a good shot."

Sarah reached up and touched the implant behind her ear with a shaky finger.

"Thanks for the warning."

She stood up and looked at the dead samurai at her feet. The AK-47 was still in his hands. Sarah wrenched it away and slipped the strap over her shoulder. Travis was talking to her again.

"Can you see the plane from up there?"

Sarah squinted and scanned the horizon. "Where's it coming from? Oh, wait. I see it." She grinned. "The cavalry has arrived!"

"All right. Get the girls down while I check on Stan. Out."

Now that she knew she wasn't about to die, Sarah noticed that bullets were still flying in her direction. She raised the AK-47 and laid down a burst of fire, then ran up to grab the rest of the girls. She had to get them out of there and find the Naloxone fast. Every minute without it was sixty seconds closer to death.

One of the girls was sobbing when she got there.

"What's wrong?" Sarah asked.

The girl shook her head and pointed at Naoko, lying peacefully on the ground.

"She not breathing."

Sarah slung her weapon and grabbed Naoko's wrist. She had a pulse, but it was weak. Sarah tipped the girl's face up and opened her mouth, pinching her nose shut. She leaned forward, put her mouth over Naoko's mouth, and blew. The girl's chest did not rise. Next to her, the other girl began to sob.

"She dead."

"No she's not," Sarah snapped. "Just be quiet and let me help her."

She leaned forward and breathed into Naoko's mouth a second time, then a third. Still nothing. Sarah grabbed the girl's tongue and pulled it forward, then tried again. This time, Naoko's chest rose slightly. Cheered, Sarah breathed into the girl's mouth again. Again, Naoko's chest rose and fell.

After a minute, Sarah paused. Naoko was breathing on her own again; but she was still unconscious. She lifted the girl's eyelids—her pupils had constricted to pinpoints. They were running out of time. Unless the team wanted to go home with six dead girls, she had to get the Naloxone now.

"Travis, this is Sarah. I've got trouble. One girl in a coma and more to come if I don't get the antidote. Over."

"Roger that. The antidote's at base camp."

"Where's base camp?"

"Underground. We found Kuribayashi's bunker. You have to go through a tunnel to get there."

"Tell me where. I'll go get it."

"Negative. We've got a tango in the hole and Jennifer's trailing him. Until the place is secure, I can't risk it."

"And we can't risk losing the girls."

There was a pause. Then Travis said:

"I've got an idea. Let me talk to Stan for a minute. In the meantime, see if you can raise Sam and tell him to have the antidote ready. Out."

Sarah pulled Naoko into a sitting position and lifted her onto her shoulders in a fireman's carry. Then she grabbed the other girl's hand and pulled her to her feet. As the two of them staggered back down the cone, she listened to the men's conversation.

"Stan, this is Travis. Time to stop playing with these guys. Any way you can get a grenade over here?"

Stan sounded doubtful. "I can do it; but without a laser to guide them, they're going to go ballistic."

"Roger. We haven't got a choice. Sarah's got a girl on the ropes and she'll lose the rest if we don't do something fast. Even if a grenade doesn't kill them, the samurai'll scatter when it hits. That should be enough for me to pick off the rest."   .

"Unless you're in the line of fire."

"That's a risk I'll have to take."

Chapter Forty-seven

August 23, 0606 hours,
above the East Boat Basin, Iwo Jima

The cloud cover was thinning. As Hunter dropped the plane down toward the water, Jack watched the sub through his binoculars.

"They're getting inside. Do something!"

"Like what? I'm pushing this crate as hard as I can."

Jack pressed his lips together. He had his XM-29 rifle across his lap. If they could just get close enough, he could open the door and start shooting. But the men in the Zodiac were moving too fast. By the time the plane got there, they'd be closing the hatch.

"I've got an idea." He unzipped his jacket.

Hunter looked at him. "What?"

"Take it down. I'm gonna jump."

"Are you crazy?"

Jack pulled his shoes off and threw them into the back. "How else are we going to stop them?"

Hunter nodded. "I'll get as close as I can."

The plane dove for the water as Jack perched on the edge of his seat. He could see the men in the Zodiac scrambling out into the sub.

Come on!

The plane slowed as it neared the water.

"I can't take her below stall speed," Hunter warned. "I'll tell you when to jump. After you're out, I'll bring her around and land."

Jack nodded, keeping his eyes on the water. The engines' whine sounded like air being let out of a balloon.

"Ready?"

Jack reached for the handle. Down on the water, the last man was climbing out of the Zodiac.

"Go!"

Jack shoved the door open and jumped.

The water closed over Jack's head like hands clapping together. Jack held his breath and looked around. The sub was only fifty meters away. He kicked his way to the surface and started swimming.

The last man was through the hatch now. Jack put on a burst of speed and grabbed for the railing just as the door slammed shut. He pulled himself out of the water and ran along the spine of the submarine to the hatch. Falling to his knees, he seized the door and tried to pry it open. It was useless. The hatch was closed and secure. There was no way to force it open.

Jack pounded on the metal hull with his fists.

"Come out of there, you motherfuckers! Come out and fight!"

Then the sub began to move. Jack stood as the super-structure shuddered and started to submerge. Water rushed up over his feet and sucked at his legs. A minute later, the sail disappeared and Jack was left treading water.

Then he heard the buzz of the amphib's engines. The Goose was in the water, coming toward him. Jack waved as the plane approached. Hunter opened the door and he pulled himself inside.

"I lost her," Jack said dejectedly. "The mission's fucked."

Hunter shook his head. "No it isn't. We've still got the hedgehogs."

Jack's eyes widened. "Travis said he wanted the sho-gun alive."

"He also said we had to find out what this was all about. If the sub goes, the truth goes with it. I'll take her up and you arm the bombs. When I make a pass, you drop them overboard. We'll interrogate the survivors."

"Do you think they'll work?"

"Brad said they would."

"Yeah, in 1945! He said the plane was in good shape, too."

Hunter raised an eyebrow. "You got any better ideas?"

Jack shook his head. "Let's do it."

Jack stepped back between the seats as the plane took off again. He unwrapped the tarp and rolled out the hedgehogs. The things weighed about forty pounds apiece and looked like elongated bowling pines. A small propeller in the tail acted as a delaying mechanism to keep the bombs from detonating prematurely. Jack sat down cross-legged, set the first bomb in his lap, and licked his lips. Jesus, this thing was old. What if he tried to arm it and the damned thing went off? Hell of a way to go, blowing your own dick off. He gripped the tail and turned.

There was a switch inside. No markings to indicate what it meant, but there wasn't any time to find out. Jack flipped the switch and screwed the lid back on.

Hunter glanced back over his shoulder. "Is it armed?"

"It's whatever it wasn't before." Jack put his hand on the door and unlatched it. "Where's the sub?"

"Dead ahead. I'll let you know when to drop her."

The plane banked right and Jack felt the weight shift in his lap.

"Hold on, Jack! We're going down."

"I've only got one of them armed!"

"Maybe we'll only need one! Hang on to the other in case we miss on this pass!"

"Roger!" Jack secured the unarmed hedgehog under the tarp and wedged the live one in next to his rucksack. Then he put his shoulder to the door and pushed. With the wind whipping by, it took all his strength to force it open.

"Ready?"

"Ready!" He spun the delay timer.

Jack held the smooth gray bomb at arm's length, vertical to the water.

"Tell me when to drop it!"

"Now!"

Jack released the hedgehog and watched it drop away

as the plane surged forward and up. He let go of the door and it slammed shut.

Jack jumped to his feet and scrambled back into the cockpit. "Did we hit him?"

"I can't tell."

The plane finished a short climb, then banked right again and headed back toward the sub.

"Nothing's happening!"

"Give it a second!"

Several seconds passed with no sign of detonation.

"Did it go off?"

"I don't think so."

"Fuck!" Jack got out of his seat. "I'm arming the other one."

"Good idea."

Hunter banked again and brought the plane around as Jack unwrapped the second bomb and armed it. As Jack forced the door open, he searched the water below for any sign of the sub.

"Where'd he go?"

"Don't worry! I can still make him out."

Jack spun the propeller. "Ready when you are!"

The plane swooped and salt air rushed up at Jack, fluttering his eyelids. He pictured himself on the beach with Sergeant Striker again, making his assault on Mount Suribachi. What the hell was he doing up in the air instead of on the ground?

Hunter's voice was hoarse. *"Drop it!"*

Jack unclenched his fist and watched the hedgehog drop away. It was their last hope. If this didn't work, the mission was lost.

Jack staggered back to his seat and pressed his face to the window. Where was that Jap sub, anyway? The sea seemed calm. Too calm. He held his breath. Then suddenly, a flash of light illuminated the ocean below them and the water boiled.

"Got him!" Jack yelled.

"Yee-ha!"

As the two men watched, the sub surfaced. The hatch flew open and men swarmed out, followed by a billowing cloud of smoke. Then the shogun appeared. His headdress had come off and his red robes were on fire, but Jack recognized him immediately.

Up on the deck, the shogun threw himself into the sea and began foundering. The rest of the men were swimming to shore. No one seemed to notice his cries for help.

"Oh shit!" Hunter yelled. "I don't think he can swim."

"That's okay," Jack said. "I can."

Chapter Forty-eight

Jen staggered blindly forward, leaving a trail of blood in her wake. The ATMP had failed to stanch the flow from the wound in her arm. She felt lightheaded, almost giddy, as she made her way toward base camp. The way ahead was a haze of gray and black. She wiped her face. How far was the bunker now? It was hard to tell. She felt weak. Her landmarks were gone. How many feeder tunnels had she passed? She gripped her rifle tighter and turned another corner.

There it was. The shaft of light coming from the tunnel where she'd found the skull. Base camp was only another hundred yards away. She gritted her teeth and shook herself. She would not fail. The team was counting on her.

She tried to think. The only place to go from there was straight down to the bunker—and Sam. The tango was in front of her—she was sure of that—so, why hadn't she heard any gunshots? If the intruder had made it to the bunker, wouldn't he and Sam have exchanged rounds? Sam wasn't regular military, but he was trained to handle a weapon. If a tango had shown up, he would have defended the base camp. Wouldn't he? She shook her head again, trying to clear the cobwebs from her brain. If only she could get some fresh air, she thought, she'd be able to figure out what was going on.

As she passed the feeder tunnel, the ground began to slope away from her. Jennifer staggered ahead, her weapon in her hands, no longer able to think about anything else but getting to Sam.

Secure the base, she thought. *After that, you can worry about the rest.*

The door to the bunker was open. Jen crouched and approached it cautiously. The thermal viewer didn't show anyone inside, but she wasn't close enough to see everything yet. As she stepped closer, her finger was on the trigger.

The bunker was empty.

Jennifer stepped inside and looked around. The supplies were there, so was her wet suit; but Sam and his PowerBook were gone. She blinked, her brain fuzzy. What could have happened to him? Had he heard her warning and left before the bad guy came? Or had the tango shown up and taken him hostage? She lowered the muzzle of the M-16 and tried to think. She was so tired. If only she could sit down.

Then she heard the click of an AK-47 being cocked. She turned and saw a gap-toothed samurai with a grin on his face. His weapon was pointed right at her.

Sam had been sulking in the bunker when Jennifer's message came through. Garbled and weak, it didn't convey more than a few words; but those few words were enough. There was a tango in the hole heading for base camp!

He grabbed his head and looked around.

"Okay, don't panic. What's your situation?" Sam's eyes scanned the room.

"I've got no comnet, no power, a broken ankle . . ." He grinned. "And a Baretta nine millimeter. Good. The odds are in my favor."

Sam closed the PowerBook and picked up the gun, pleased that the pain in his ankle had been suddenly dulled.

"Thank you, Mother Nature," he whispered as adrenaline poured into his bloodstream.

He rolled onto his side and got to his knees. Jen's samurai would be here any minute. If Sam waited in the bunker, he'd be a sitting duck. He had to get away, but where?

Sam froze as a burst of machine gun fire echoed in the tunnel. There wasn't time to think about it; he had to get moving *now*. Five feet into the tunnel was an old rifle. Rusted and useless for fighting, it was perfect for Sam. He grabbed the stock, turned it on end and used it as a cane to steady himself as he hobbled off into the unknown.

Thank goodness he had his helmet on. Sam reached up and slapped down the visor, using the BSD's thermal sensors to guide him through the darkened passageway. Another burst of machine gun fire made him jump, but he kept going. If the bad guy showed up, Sam would see him coming before he saw Sam. If not, he'd find a place to wait it out while Jen flushed the guy.

The tunnel turned and started to level out. Sam breathed a sigh of relief. Going uphill had started his ankle throbbing again.

"I guess even Mother Nature has her limits," he muttered.

Ten yards ahead, Sam saw a shaft of light. It was the tunnel where Jen found the skull! Could he slip in there and wait? Doubtful. The light would give his opponent a clear shot. Sam was a decent marksman, but it never hurt to have the element of surprise on your side. He struggled forward, lost his balance, and fell sideways.

Right through the wall of the tunnel.

"What the hell?"

Sam reached out and groped the small, cobweb-filled depression. It wasn't a tunnel, but clearly, someone had been digging here. The area carved out of the rock was about the size of a steamer trunk—perfect for a guy Sam's size—and no one would ever think to find him there. He sat down with his back to the indentation and pulled his feet in behind him. Perfect.

Sam propped the Baretta between his knees and glared down the barrel.

"Go ahead," he whispered. "Make my day."

There were sounds in the tunnel now. Sam pressed his back into the rock and listened. Someone was coming. His breath became shallow and tight. Who was it? Jen or the other guy? He didn't dare fire if there was any doubt. No. If it was one of the team, they'd have a happy homecoming. If not, better to let Jen take care of him.

The noises got louder and Sam could make out footsteps in the littered passageway. He gripped the Baretta's barrel as sweat ran down his face.

Oh God, please don't let him see me.

Someone stepped past. A blur in Sam's vision, quickly gone. Not a TALON. He gulped.

Don't worry. Jen's coming. Just hold tight.

When a minute passed and Jen didn't show, Sam's imagination went into overdrive. What if there was more than one bad guy out there? What if that burst of gunfire had been for Jen? What if the mission had failed and Sam was the only TALON left alive?

He heard footsteps again, but this time they were coming from the bunker.

Shit! What happened to Jen?

The bogey stepped past, never even glancing at Sam, and headed for the feeder tunnel up ahead. Sam closed his eyes.

Jen, where are you?

Then he saw her: hunched over, she lurched past him like a drunk. Sam frowned. What was wrong with her? Hadn't she seen that guy in the tunnel? Or was he gone by now? Damn! He wished there was some way he could talk to her. Some way that didn't make noise, that is.

There was another noise in the tunnel. The bad guy was coming back! Crouched, gun at the ready, he slipped by Sam like a shadow across the moon. Sam watched him follow Jen to the bunker and felt a little better. Jen was no slouch. She'd hear that motherfucker from a mile away and blow him to bits.

Then he saw the blood.

A smear on the wall where Jen had passed. Sam leaned forward and brought it into focus. *Was* it blood? It had to be. What else would come off her clothing and stain the tunnel walls?

There was no time to figure it out. If Jen was hurt then

that guy behind her could kill her. Sam pulled himself to his feet and hobbled down the tunnel after them.

Jen stared at the muzzle of the AK-47. Her brain was too fuzzy to register the danger. She knew she was going to die. It made sense. Death came out of a gun's muzzle. But for the life of her, she couldn't figure out what to do about it. Her legs and arms were so weak. If only she could just sit down and rest.

The man yelled something at her in Japanese and she felt like laughing. Did she look Japanese to this guy? Did the Japs even have any women in combat? Where the hell did he think these hooters came from? She felt giddy as the little asshole kept spouting off.

Then he stopped talking. Jen saw his finger tighten on the trigger.

Oh well, she thought, *at least I died young and beautiful.*

The shot rang out. Jen looked around, wondering when she'd realize she was dead. So far, nothing much was happening. She looked up. The ugly little samurai was lying on the floor with a fountain of blood spurting from his head.

"Wow," she said stupidly. "Good trick."

Then Sam stepped into the room, took one look at the guy on the floor and threw up all over her. Jen wrinkled her nose and turned away.

"Oh, Sam," she drawled as she passed out. "You ruined everything."

Chapter Forty-nine

Jack opened the door and crouched, watching the water, waiting for the plane to pass over the shogun. As much as he hated to save the guy, he knew that the team—especially he and Hunter—would be in deep shit if the shogun died. This whole thing was such a fuck-up.

Jack took a deep breath and jumped into the water again. He broke the surface and started paddling.

The shogun was gasping and splashing about fifteen feet ahead. It was clear from his movements that he couldn't swim; but so far, none of his men had come back to help him. The sub was nowhere in sight.

Jack hesitated. Saving a drowning man was a tricky operation. In desperation, people often grabbed onto their would-be rescuers and took them both under. The trick was to approach the person while keeping his arms away from you—preferably without his knowing it. The shogun hadn't spotted him yet; but if Jack swam toward him, he would. The only way to approach this guy was from the bottom. Jack took a deep breath and dove.

The water was incredibly clear. As Jack swam forward underwater, it was as if he was paddling through air.

The shogun was directly overhead now. Jack saw his feet kicking aimlessly and his arms flailing, barely keeping the man's head above water. Jack flipped onto his back and lined his body up beneath the shogun's. When he ascended, Jack would have to go straight up the guy's spine, grab him around the neck, and start swimming for shore before he knew what hit him. Your average drowning victim would relax and stop struggling once he found his face above water. But this guy wasn't your average victim. If he put up a fight, Jack would just have to apply more pressure on the guy's neck until he decided to cooperate. In this much water, there was no room for compromise.

Jack stretched out his arms and gave one mighty kick, rocketing himself upward. As his face broke the surface, he looped his left arm around the shogun's neck, tilted the man's face up, and began a modified sidestroke with his right arm, moving his feet in a scissors kick.

The man's struggles ceased almost immediately. Jack breathed a sigh of relief as he felt the shogun relax and allow himself to be towed to shore. As best as Jack could tell, they were about a quarter mile from the beach.

By the time Jack's feet touched the shore, he was exhausted. Lack of food, sleep, and water had combined with the sheer physical exertion of dragging another man through the water. He pulled the shogun up onto the beach and laid him out. The man was breathing, but apparently unconscious. No matter. He was alive and that's all that mattered.

Then Jack collapsed, his clothes waterlogged and heavy. His head was swimming and his body was weak; but he smiled, relieved. He'd done it. Stopped the sub and rescued the shogun. The mission was secure. Now all they had to do was interrogate the guy and find out what this was all about.

He raised up on one elbow. The shogun was kneeling in the sand, bent forward, his hands clasped in front of him as he murmured something in Japanese. Then Jack saw something shiny in the guy's hands—a knife.

My God, the guy's going to commit hari kari!

"No!" Jack screamed. He threw himself forward and plowed into the man, knocking him over and sending black sand in all directions.

The shogun rolled away and scrambled for the knife. Jack flew at him, trying to get control of the weapon, but the shogun had it first. He grabbed the knife and rolled away, then stood and brandished it at Jack.

Jack got to this feet just as the man lunged, knife in hand. He staggered back and fell as the blade whizzed past his chest. The shogun turned quickly and slashed at him a second time. Jack had no time to recover. He dodged the knife and lost his balance again. He hit the sand with a bone-crunching thud.

This guy was good! But what the hell was he so mad about? Jack was just trying to save his life. Jack scrambled away and got to one knee. From this position, he'd be able to launch himself forward if the guy came at him again. If he could avoid the thrust of the blade, he'd be okay. A slash wound would heal.

The shogun was on his feet, circling Jack, waiting for an opportunity to strike. Jack swallowed, waiting for him to make the first move.

When the strike of a hawk breaks the body of its prey, it is because of timing.

Jack moved to the right, keeping the distance between the two of them constant. Now, the two of them were circling one another, neither man gaining—or losing—his advantage. Jack wished to God he had a knife. Or that the shogun was a less-skilled opponent. Skill and superior weaponry put him in control of the situation. Jack would simply have to wait him out.

Then Jack heard something. A buzzing noise that was rapidly growing louder. The shogun's eyes widened and Jack grinned.

"Surprise surprise," he cackled.

Jack ducked as Hunter flew up behind the shogun and passed overhead. When the terrified Jap turned to see what the racket was about, Jack made his move.

He lunged forward, grabbing the shogun's hand. The man fought him, turning the blade toward Jack's face and redoubling his effort. Jack's arm was shaking. His strength was nearly gone.

The tip of the knife was only inches from his eye. Jack dug his toes into the sand and struggled forward, pushing the shogun's hand up and away from his face with both hands, forcing the knife away.

Then Jack pivoted, driving his shoulder into the man's chin, and brought the shogun's arm down in front of him. He twisted the man's hand and heard a snap. The shogun screamed and dropped the knife. Then Jack yanked—hard—up and over while he drove his body back into the other man's. The shogun flew off his feet and tumbled over Jack's shoulder, hitting the packed sand. Jack pushed him away with his foot and retrieved the knife.

"Jack!"

He turned. Travis was running across the flatland with Stan barreling down the path after him.

Travis threw an arm around Jack and hugged him.

"Good work!"

"Yeah, nice job," Stan said.

"Thanks." Jack licked his lips. "Damn! That sucker almost killed himself."

"We saw," Travis said. "You were brilliant."

Stan's eyes glinted. "Man, when you were struggling with that guy, fighting to push the knife away and all, you looked like that picture of the Marines raising the flag on Suribachi. It was beautiful."

Jack looked around. "Where's everybody else?"

"Sam's in the bunker with a broken ankle. Hunter's got the plane in the water. I told him to wait offshore until we had the beach secured."

"The girls?"

"They're okay. Sarah gave each of them an injection of Naloxone and it looks like they'll pull through."

Jack wavered. He felt lightheaded. His knees were weak. "How about—" He swallowed. "How about Jen?"

Travis's face was grave. "One of the tangos shot her. Sarah's taking care of her in the bunker. She's lost a lot of blood, but I swapped battery arrays with her and the ATMP's got her stabilized until Sarah can stitch her up." He reached out. "You okay?"

Jack was going to say yes. He meant to. But when he opened his mouth, his legs collapsed and he found himself sitting on the beach.

"Yeah. I'm okay," he said feebly. "Just thirsty, that's all. I haven't had any water since, since . . ."

"Here," Stan said. "I refilled my canteen after I came off the volcano." He handed it to Jack, who took it gratefully. "Don't drink it too fast. You'll puke it all up again."

Jack smiled weakly and took a sip. "Tastes good."

"Piss tastes good if you're thirsty enough."

Jack took another sip and looked up at the volcano, smoking in the distance. "What was that guy trying to do, anyway? Commit Harry Carey or something?"

"It's *hara-kiri*, Big Dude. And the Japanese prefer the term *seppuku*." Everyone turned as Sam hobbled up behind them on a makeshift crutch. "Hara-kiri literally means 'to cut the stomach,'" Sam informed them. He shook his head. "Too vulgar. When a samurai cuts his stomach open with a knife, he does it to maintain his honor. The word seppuku denotes an honorable death."

"But why would he try to kill himself?" Jack asked.

Travis looked at the shogun, lying in the sand, subdued and despondent. "Maybe we should ask him." He grabbed the man's shirt and pulled him to his feet.

There was an audible gasp from Sam. "My God!" he said. "It's Iguchi Tanaka!"

Epilogue

It was a balmy 74 degrees in Maui. Blue sky, sunshine, and miles of ocean beyond the slender strip of sand. The babes were hot and the beer was cold.

Stan looked around and smiled. "This is the life."

Sarah sucked some beer from her bottle and broke the suction with a satisfying smack. "How so?"

"Angela's four thousand miles away figuring out how to spend my TALON hazard pay and I'm here, brew in hand, eyeing the surfer chicks." He squinted behind his Foster Grants. "Let's see. Which one deserves me?"

Sarah rolled her eyes. "None of them *deserves* you. At least, no more than they deserve the plague."

Stan ignored her. "Yeah, there's nothing like mission accomplished to make a man feel horny."

"Mission accomplished minus one. We lost one girl, remember?"

Stan scoffed. "Okay, we lost one girl. But we straightened out the Japs, didn't we?"

"That we did," Sarah agreed. "Did you hear the prime minister resigned?"

"Like he had any choice. When General Krauss and the entire National Security Council saw Tanaka's face on their satellite feed in the War Room at the Pentagon, they sent a tape of the whole operation to the president. TALON's comnet paid for itself this time."

"Suppose we'll get our trade agreement now?"

"Already been signed, sealed, and delivered. *And* I

think we can pretty much forget about Tanaka's samurai making any more trouble. They're all cooling their heels in neat little Jap jails now."

"Sam tell you that?"

"Who else?" Stan pointed with his beer bottle. "Travis sure is having a good time."

Sarah glanced down the beach at the towel where Travis and Maggie were making out.

"He's been dry humping that broad since we got here." Stan cupped a hand around his mouth and yelled at them. "You know what Nike says, Trav. Just *do* it!" He turned to Sarah. "Don't know what he's wasting his time on her for."

"What's the matter with her? I think Maggie's nice."

"Too tall, too made-up, too tough." Stan counted Maggie's liabilities on his fingers. "And too much lip. Did you hear the ration of shit she gave me about the girl from Wahini Lei's that I hosed last week? Shit, was it *my* fault she thought I loved her?" He shook his head. "Jesus, women are dumb."

Sarah turned her head to look at Jen, who was amusing herself by flirting with a blonde body builder in a turquoise Speedo.

Stan followed her gaze. "That guy's as queer as a three dollar bill."

"What makes you think that?"

"Look at him! What's he wearing, makeup or something? The guy must spend an hour doing his hair."

Jen laughed at something the guy said and Stan shook his head.

"What the hell does she see in all that muscle, anyway? Only muscle that counts on a man is the one between his legs." Stan looked at Sarah. "Can I ask you something? Just between us, I mean."

"Sure."

"Are you a lez?"

Sarah's laugh was short and explosive. "What?!"

"Well, are you?"

"Why? Because I don't drag my tongue on the ground every time you walk by?"

He paused. "Basically . . . yeah."

Sarah shook her head. "You amaze me, you know that? You are the most conceited asshole I've ever met."

"You didn't answer my question."

"The answer's no, Stan. *Emphatically* no."

Stan looked pleased. "So, you want to take a ride on the old hump-a-lump some time?"

"Sorry, babe. You're not my type."

Sarah looked around for Jack and Hunter. The two of them had spent the morning playing sand volleyball and reliving their ordeal on Asuncion, but she'd lost sight of them when Stan joined her.

"Wonder what Jack and Hunter are up to?"

"Getting drunk, I hope."

Sarah spotted them. "There they are."

The two TALONs were playing Frisbee with a pair of girls in string bikinis who looked like they were on semester break. From the looks they were getting from the coeds, those two wouldn't be tossing that plastic saucer around for long.

"Is Sam doing okay?"

"Yeah. I left him back at the hotel. He said his ankle hurt too much to walk in the sand."

"Hope he's all right."

"Yeah, me too. We just got the little twerp broken in."

A pert blonde in a pink thong bikini walked in front of them. Stan lifted his sunglasses, inspecting the view, and whistled softly. The girl turned her head and winked at him over her shoulder.

"That's my cue, Toots," he said, setting his beer in the sand. "Catch you later."

Sarah watch him go, feeling relieved. Stan could be fun in small doses, but right now she felt like she'd OD'd on the guy. Still, he had been company. It wasn't much fun sitting on the beach alone. She scuffed her toe in the warm sand and wiggled it between her toes.

"Sarah?"

She looked up, shielding her eyes from the sun as she studied the face of the young man in front of her. His black hair had streaks of green on the top and he had a tattoo of a rose around his belly button. He'd just stepped out of the surf. The water was still dripping off his baggy shorts.

"Josh?"

He hunkered down and put his hands on his knees, bobbing his head enthusiastically.

"You remember me!"

Sarah bit her lip. Remember him? How could she forget him? The kid was ten years her junior and had twice the energy she did between the sheets. The last time they'd seen each other had been on the slopes in Stowe, Vermont, ripping down the snow on their well-waxed boards.

"What are you doing here?" she asked. "I thought you were strictly a snow monkey."

He laughed and pushed a lock of dripping hair out of his eyes.

"Hey, the cold gets old. Where you staying? Maybe we can get together." He grinned hopefully.

"Sounds good. I'll give you the phone number of the hotel." Sarah reached for her backpack and pulled out a pencil and a piece of paper. "It's been a long time."

"Yeah, it has. What have you been up to lately?"

Sarah cracked a knowing smile and handed him the phone number.

"You'd never believe it if I told you."

The Explosive New Military Action Series

N A V Y   S E A L S

MIKE MURRAY

**Navy SEAL unit Mobile 4 does not exist...
The U.S. Military does not acknowledge them...
The White House has never heard of them...
And no one who has ever seen them in action
has lived to tell about them....**

__NAVY SEALS: INSURRECTION RED

                           0-451-19946-4/$5.99

__NAVY SEALS: BLACKLIGHT

                           0-451-19971-5/$5.99

__NAVY SEALS: GREEN SOLITAIRE

                           0-451-20050-0/$5.99

PENGUIN PUTNAM INC.
Online

Your Internet gateway to a virtual environment with
hundreds of entertaining and enlightening books
from Penguin Putnam Inc.

*While you're there, get the latest buzz on
the best authors and books around—*

Tom Clancy, Patricia Cornwell, W.E.B. Griffin,
Nora Roberts, William Gibson, Robin Cook,
Brian Jacques, Catherine Coulter, Stephen King,
Jacquelyn Mitchard, and many more!

**Penguin Putnam Online is located at
http://www.penguinputnam.com**

PENGUIN PUTNAM NEWS

Every month you'll get an inside look at our upcom-
ing books and new features on our site. This is an
ongoing effort to provide you with the most
up-to-date information about
our books and authors.

**Subscribe to Penguin Putnam News at
http://www.penguinputnam.com/ClubPPI**